"Was Raven here, standing in my way, simply because I was the shiny thing that fell out of the elves' pocket? All her talk of deals suggested she was more interested in playing than in helping.…"

ELF RAISED

NORTHERN CREATURES BOOK THREE

KRIS AUSTEN RADCLIFFE

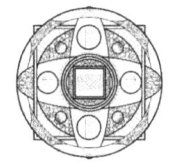

THE WORLDS OF
KRIS AUSTEN RADCLIFFE

Smart Urban Fantasy:

Northern Creatures

Monster Born

Vampire Cursed

Elf Raised

Wolf Hunted

Fae Touched

Death Kissed

God Forsaken

Magic Scorned

Witch Burned (*coming soon*)

Northern Creatures Box Set One: Books 1-3

Northern Creatures Box Set Two: Books 4-6

Genre-bending Science Fiction about
love, family, and dragons:

WORLD ON FIRE

Series one

Fate Fire Shifter Dragon

Games of Fate

Flux of Skin

Fifth of Blood

Bonds Broken & Silent

All But Human

Men and Beasts

The Burning World

Dragon's Fate and Other Stories

Hot Contemporary Romance:

ELF RAISED

NORTHERN CREATURES
Book Three

By
Kris Austen Radcliffe

Six Talon Sign Fantasy & Futuristic Romance
Minneapolis

www.krisaustenradcliffe.com

ELF RAISED

CHAPTER 1

Sometimes, I wonder if time has the same physicality as space. It's a strange thought, especially for a man who lives inside Alfheim's magical bubble, but the world's not all elves and vampires. It's not all witches and ghosts and Lands of both Living and Dead.

I'm the cobbled-together son of a mad scientist, and sometimes a scientific point of view helps me to understand a situation better than magic.

I stood in my underwear on the deck between my house and the lake. I'd come out to warm my corpse-cold body in the bright morning sun, partly because I didn't like my post-sleep, creaky aches, and partly because Benta wouldn't touch me until my flesh felt living once again.

Benta the Nameless, the elf who also happened to be my ex, had decided the previous evening that "ex" was a relative descriptor, and had stayed the night.

Benta made coffee inside. And outside, a woman I did not know—a beautiful woman with auburn-red hair and a bright, keen face—ran down the path toward my deck.

I did not know her, but she knew me. The way she watched me and navigated the path, and the way my dog circled her legs as she moved, telegraphed that this woman understood my house and property. My canine emperor, Marcus Aurelius, trusted her. And she was carrying my backpack.

"Frank!" she called.

Somewhere in the back of my mind—somewhere in the distant topography of memory or time or whatever currents we all swim against every single moment of our lives—I heard a call.

Remember, it said.

"Who are you?" I asked. I didn't know this woman but I wanted to. I wanted to pick her up and spend the day touching and talking and laughing together.

She had my backpack. She had my dog. And she looked happy to see cold, creaky me.

"Ellie Jones," she said. "The concealment enchantments wipe your memory every night." She hugged me.

A woman I did not know but did—she was familiar in the way a land's colors are familiar. In the way animal calls and bird chirps let you know you're in a certain part of the forest or near a river because only this part of the world sounds and smells this way.

Ellie Jones was that kind of familiar. I understood her touch, even if I did not recognize it.

"I'm your—"

Benta walked out onto the deck in her full, mostly-naked, elf glory, with coffee in hand and her attention on my wayward dog.

The woman named Ellie Jones dropped her hand from my chest and I swear all the cold of the Arctic returned to my bones. All the isolation and the howling wind. All the aimless wandering. My soul moved from the life-filled wonder that was a summer with Ellie Jones to the winter desolation I left behind long, long ago.

Remember, that distant voice called.

Ellie stared at Benta. Her mouth closed. She pulled my phone from her pocket and set it on the deck's railing.

She picked up my backpack. "I'm sorry," she said, and turned away.

I should understand where to map Ellie Jones into my world. I should comprehend why I wanted to follow—and to orbit. She'd caught my soul in her gravity well.

Marcus Aurelius looked to me. He wagged his tail. Then he looked over his shoulder at Ellie as she vanished up the path.

He barked.

Remember, whispered again through my mind.

"Go," I said, and pointed at the path. "Protect." I wanted to say *Protect Ellie*, but her name wouldn't come out.

Ellie's concealments interacted with elves and I was standing in the eye of the storm. I *knew*, though I didn't remember learning what I knew. Benta's magical elven proximity messed with my ability to articulate my thoughts.

My dog understood. He barked again and ran after the woman named Ellie Jones whom I should remember.

"Thank you," I whispered.

Benta stretched her neck. "Where's Marcus Aurelius going?" She sipped her coffee, but didn't seem all that distressed that my dog had come home only to immediately leave again.

"He'll be back," I said. Maybe. If he never came home again, at least I knew he was with someone who cared about him. I knew the same way I knew Benta's proximity interfered with my ability to speak of Ellie Jones.

But...

My dog was okay. I was okay. I'd survived a magical, soul- and blood-siphoning pike through my chest and now I had a naked Benta the Nameless standing on my deck looking at me as if she disapproved of how long it took the sun to warm my cold flesh.

I really should be remembering something—someone. I rubbed my forehead. Sometimes the surreal nature of my life popped a jab right into my face.

Benta brushed her fingers along my thigh as she walked toward my phone, which was sitting on my deck railing for some reason that, again, I did not remember.

She set down her coffee and picked up the device. "Did you leave this out here?" She handed it to me.

I stared at the phone wondering if I should unlock it and check my messages. Arne wanted me to come into The Great Hall. Most everyone who knew about magic would be coming into The Hall today, one way or the other.

When the elves did a magical reset, debriefing always followed, and my debriefing would include hours of discussion about what happened in the now-closed pocket borderland where the elves had trapped a horde of vampires.

A horde, and my fully, finally, utterly dissociated vampire brother.

No more Lord Dracula for the universe, or so we hoped. *I* hoped. But a contingency plan needed forming, because only fools left behind an ash-filled, unguarded pocket borderland full of magic-wielding vampires.

But right now, I wanted to warm my cold bones. And Benta, it seemed, wanted to help.

Yet I could not shake the feeling that entire kingdoms within the Realms of Time were shrouded from my perception. That entire sections of my map of the past had gone missing and now I had no idea how to navigate the future.

Fog lurked out there. And monsters. Maybe dragons, too. And here I stood on my deck in my underwear.

I handed the phone to Benta. "Take this in, would you?" I asked. "I'll warm up."

She carefully kissed my cheek—even though she'd been lightly touching, major contact wouldn't happen until I came inside.

Somewhere deep in the back of my mind, from that unknown kingdom inside the hidden realms of time, a voice called out. That barely-perceptible call to pay attention to things other than what was right under my nose. To put my energy into making sure that I truly did understand the world around me.

Remember, it said. But what? I had no idea.

Benta sniffed the air as if she smelled a hint of dead animal—or danger. She shook her head and wrapped her arms around her breasts as if the morning air suddenly chilled her radiant elf skin.

She took my phone. Then Benta the Nameless walked away.

I looked out over the path that led from my deck into the trees. Maybe I should get dressed and go look for my dog. Or maybe I should warm up and go debrief the Elf King of Alfheim.

I sipped my coffee. Arne first. At least I could map that bit of the past.

CHAPTER 2

Benta was in the shower when I walked into the kitchen. Water rushed through the pipes, and the sounds of her knocking around shampoo bottles echoed through my house. She sang too, and the occasional sonic wonder of sung Icelandic filtered through the walls.

I set my mug on the counter and stretched my shoulders. The sun and the coffee had helped, and my morning cold creaks and aches had settled into my normal large and lumbering.

Benta launched into a shower rendition of a pop song I recognized —still in Icelandic, but the melody was unmistakable—and I shook my head. I had a beautiful singing elf in my shower.

What a strange life I lived.

Time to dress. Time to make my way to The Great Hall. All the vampire business needed settling once and for all.

I walked into the bedroom and rooted around in my dresser for a clean pair of jeans and a fresh t-shirt. I pulled out my prized "Alfheim Gossiping Squirrels" Sprouts League baseball jersey—Jaxson Geroux's team had won their version of Regionals last spring—complete with its bold "Champion" letters and its mean, bat-wielding Ratatoskr mascot. The kid had proudly handed out the shirts to every adult he knew, and had made a point of ordering one in my size. No way could I have said no. Not that any sane person would pass up a "Gossiping Squirrels" t-shirt, anyway.

The water shut off just as a vehicle pulled into my driveway. I tucked in my t-shirt and glanced out the bedroom window.

Maura parked a brand-new, deep red, one-ton truck in front of my garage. It rumbled like a big cat, and dropped smoothly into silence when she turned it off.

Akeyla Maurasdottir bounded out of the passenger side and ran for the front door.

Maura had said something about moving back in this weekend. She said nothing about buying a new truck.

I rounded the corner into the hallway. "Maura and Akeyla are here!" I called.

"Okay," Benta responded through the bathroom door.

Best not to freak out my little niece with a naked houseguest, especially since Benta was one of her grandmother's friends.

The doorbell rang. I opened the door.

"Uncle Frank!" Akeyla launched herself at me. "Mommy said the icky vampires tried to hurt you again but you and Grandpa and Grandma and Ms. Benta and Mr. Magnus stopped them and got back Mr. Magnus's big horses!"

I settled her on my hip. "That's right, honey. We stopped the icky vampires."

Out on the driveway, Maura exited the truck, as did Jaxson Geroux. He wiggled his nine-year-old shoulders like the young Alpha he was, then smiled and waved.

I waved back.

"Jax is spending the day with you?" I asked.

She hugged my neck. "His mommy and daddy have to work for Grandpa today."

"Ah," I said. Arne must have the Alphas checking the pack for residual effects of the elves' cleansing spells.

Jax watched Maura close her door. Then he scanned the trees the same way his father did when Gerard looked for threats. When Jax was satisfied, he walked to the back of the truck and waited.

Born-wolves were rare, though the few that made it through infancy tended to be the children of Alphas. But being the son of two Alphas also meant that Jax could be... intense. He was also a damned good young pitcher and likely to be recruited when he hit high school. He even looked like a kid destined for the Majors—he carried his father's French musculature on his mother's lean and fast Somali frame. He was the prototypical strong, skinny kid who we all knew would soon develop surprisingly broad shoulders.

Akeyla didn't mind Jax's intensity. If anything, her free fire spirit energy loosened up his more piercing traits.

Out on the driveway, Maura handed Jax a suitcase.

"Mr. Magnus said you helped save Bloodyhoof," Akeyla said. "Bloodyhoof is *huge*." Her eyes rounded to reflect her sense of the stallion's size.

"He is," I said.

"I want to ride Bloodyhoof but Grandpa says I have to start with the smaller horses first," she said.

I set her down. "Bloodyhoof's big even for *me*."

"No, he's not. He's just the right size for you." She shook her head as if I was being dumb Uncle Frank again.

"Mr. Magnus won't let anyone ride Bloodyhoof," Jax said as he walked up. Even at nine, he could carry a big suitcase with ease.

He set the case on the step. "I think Bloodyhoof would like Akeyla." He looked around as if once again checking for threats.

"Everything's good here, Jax," I said.

He looked up at me with an expression that was equal parts not understanding and understanding all too well. He nodded once and glanced around my leg and into the house. "Where's Marcus Aurelius?" he asked.

A dusting of magic washed over the kids as he took Akeyla's hand.

I looked at Maura. She frowned but didn't say anything as she pulled three more suitcases out of the back of the truck. Akeyla, though, swung Jax's hand as if playing a game and pulled him into the house. "Let's go down to the lake!" she said, and skipped by.

Jax looked over his shoulder. "Can we play with your dog?"

All the wolves loved my canine emperor. Even Gaupe, Arne's lynx, liked him. "He didn't come home last night," I said, though I didn't think that was quite right. "He's safe." Though I didn't know that, either.

Benta stepped out of the bathroom, thankfully fully clothed, and out of glamour with her wet yet still somehow lively ponytail waving behind her head.

"Ms. Benta!" Akeyla squealed. She let go of Jax and launched herself at the elf in much the same way she'd launched herself at me when she arrived.

Benta did not lift up Akeyla the way I had. She squatted instead and offered a hug. "Shouldn't you two be at school?"

"It's Saturday!" the kids said in unison.

Benta laughed as she hugged first Akeyla, then Jax. "I don't get to see you two out of The Great Hall." She looked Jax over. "Did you have fun at the Aquarium?"

Axlam and Maura had taken the kids to Duluth while Arne and the rest of the elves cleansed the town of vampires and vampire-caused "ickiness."

Jax shrugged. "Can we go see the cougars at your Sanctuary? The cougars are cool."

Benta patted his shoulder. "They can't rehab if there are little wolves around."

He frowned as if Benta had said the meanest thing an adult could say—which she had, in some ways. A little magic and the kid would be fine around the cats, so I didn't understand why she would dismiss him the way she did.

"Can we learn rehabbing?" Akeyla asked. "I want to learn how to help at the Sanctuary, Ms. Benta."

Jax's frown deepened. The poor kid really seemed to want to visit the cats.

Benta looked up at me and I suspect she read my response on my face. She sniffed and looked away. "I'll think about it," she said.

I opened my mouth, but out on the driveway, Maura dropped a suitcase onto the gravel. I pointed. "Back in a second," I said, and walked outside.

I'd talk to Benta about her no-wolf policy later.

Birds chirped and squirrels ran tree trunks. Maura inhaled deeply and slammed the truck's tailgate.

She smirked and held out the keys. "Special delivery."

Today, Maura wore her standard "Akeyla's Mom" glamour—brown ponytail, smooth though supposedly middle-aged face, blue eyes, large-ish breasts with matching hips. She looked like three quarters of the mundane women in Alfheim.

The truck also matched the mundanes. "When did you get a new truck?" I asked.

Maura rolled her eyes. "It's for *you*, silly." She shook her head. "A gift from Magnus to say thank you for saving his horses."

The vampires had totaled my old truck and I was, at the moment, relying on Benta for transportation. I took the keys. "*He* saved his horses, not me."

Magnus had woven the sigils that cleansed Bloodyhoof and the two Percherons of their low-demon possessions.

Maura chuckled. "I told him you'd say that. He now owes me twenty bucks."

I frowned.

"What?" she asked, then shook her head again.

The truck looked to be a newer model of the same vehicle I'd driven before the vamps destroyed it.

Maura nodded toward the cab. "Magnus says it has all the bells and whistles. It sure drives nice."

Magnus gave me a truck? Part of me wondered what he wanted in exchange. But Magnus wasn't *that* kind of elf, and had many times over the years been generous with townspeople in need.

Maura squeezed my arm. "Several elder elves were in Dad's den this morning." She glanced at the house. "They were yelling, which is why we came early. The kids don't need that."

No, they didn't. No one needed whatever political fight the elder elves were in the process of hatching.

"They want Benta to come in as soon as possible." She looked up at me. "And you."

Was the truck Magnus buttering me up for a new fight?

Maura ran her hand across the top of the truck's bed. "Magnus wants to thank you, though I do think he's binding one of Alfheim's greatest warriors to the kingdom." She rubbed her neck. "If it's conscious or not, I don't know."

"What were they yelling about?" Because if a new fight was coming, I'd like to know what it was.

She looked up at my face again. "Someone flew into The Cities last night. Magnus sent a plane down to bring them north." She looked away. "There was talk of a Conclave."

Oh, no, I thought. The last time the elves called a Conclave, they deposed one of the Kings.

Arne was vulnerable.

Maura looked down at the gravel. "It hasn't even been a full twenty-four hours since they closed up Vampland."

"Vampland?" They gave the pocket borderland a name?

Maura chuckled. "You can thank your niece for that one."

"Arne let Akeyla name the vampire's pocket land?"

"What else are we going to call it?" She shrugged. "Land of the Evil Librarians?"

She had a point.

"I'll come in." Arne needed to know what happened in Vampland, especially if he had to defend his actions to the other Kings. Not that I wanted to tell that tale, but I was the one who'd had the pipe in my chest, so it was up to me to give him the details. "Benta will when she's ready."

Maura nodded toward the house. "Are we interrupting?" she asked. "Moving back in today?"

"No," I said, probably faster than Maura expected. Benta would not be spending a lot of nights. I learned that the last time we were semi-together, though I don't think my negative response came from her attitude, but more from her being here in the first place.

I looked back at the door. The kids were leading her toward the kitchen. Though Jax still frowned, neither of them seemed upset about finding her here, so why did I feel uncomfortable?

Maura picked up one of her suitcases. "I don't want to impose," she said. "Really. I don't. If you and Benta are back together and need space, we can go back to Mom and Dad's place."

Something thumped in my kitchen. Akeyla laughed. Jax said something I couldn't hear.

They were magical, the kids. Yes, in a literal sense that coiled around them, but also in a family way—true family. I wasn't giving that up.

I didn't see Benta taking to my life well, no matter how much of a sensual mother-goddess she was.

"Come in," I said. "Benta and I aren't serious." No, we weren't. We couldn't be. "She wanted to keep an eye on me last night."

Maura snorted. "Sure, big brother." She winked as she carried her suitcase toward the door. "Whatever you say!"

I picked up my elven sister's other suitcases and carried her life back into my world.

CHAPTER 3

After lots of promises to take the kids to The Alfheim Wildcat Sanctuary for a tour and some age-appropriate volunteer training—I insisted Benta allow Jax to come—she kissed my cheek, gathered her things, and made her way into town and her elf business. I was to make my way to The Great Hall posthaste in my Magnus-gifted, shiny new truck.

Maura watched me more than Benta when the elder elf left. My adoptive sister stood in the hallway with her arms crossed and her lips thin. Then she shook her head and returned to herding magical children.

The kids wouldn't let me go until we laid out a detailed plan for this evening's dinner and brownie dessert. I left with a long grocery list and promises to bring back everything the kids needed to make "magic burgers" and "fun fries." No doubt I'd be running the grill this evening, international elven crisis or not.

Akeyla and Jax waved as I walked toward Magnus's gifted behemoth, then they ran around the house to the deck. Maura followed, but took a moment to inspect the damaged wine bottle gate.

I suspected she'd have it fixed before the end of the week.

My new truck was a dark, almost-wine shade of red and for a

second I considered naming it Bloodyhood, but thought better of it. I suspected one of the kids would also come up with the same name soon enough, anyway.

I hopped into the bed. She had the nicest bedliner I'd ever seen, with a grippy-yet-clean black finish. The new toolbox gleamed in the bright morning light. The hinge locked when I opened it, but the most impressive addition was a well-organized, already-stocked interior and a section that appeared to be specifically for my elven axe, Sal.

Someone had stuffed a soft indigo-violet velvet blanket, shimmering with a consistent low-level magic, into the space.

I'd rather know who had enchanted the blanket before I placed my axe in the toolbox, and I'd already put her on the passenger seat. She seemed fine with my decision, and I got the sense she'd rather be in the open air, anyway.

"I think you'll like your spot back here, though," I said.

She mentally shrugged. Right now, she liked the idea of riding shotgun.

"Whatever you want, my friend," I said.

The impression my axe threw back at me was *That's right.* I laughed and closed the toolbox.

The impressiveness of the interior matched the exterior—Bloodyhood was a lovely piece of machinery, with soft leather seats, individual temperature controls on the vents, heads-up displays for function and monitor, and at least six cup holders. The vent controls were a bit much, but I expected nothing less from Magnus.

I drove through downtown to get a look at the site where the vampires had yanked me into Vampland. The intersection was still blocked off, and I suspected Ed Martinez, our sheriff, had towed what was left of my old truck to Gullinbursti's.

I turned onto the service road fronting The Great Hall. I'd check to see if Ed had left me a message once I parked.

The Great Hall looked... different. The elves' cleansing spells reset all glamours, and the "dingy hotel" default still looked dingy, but something had shifted.

I parked in the real lot across the street, in the back corner where my new truck wouldn't be in the way, and stared at the hotel façade the elves use to keep mundanes out of their business.

The building hadn't changed—it continued to look like a beige-painted concrete box with a party space slapped onto its side. The "parking lot" buffer wasn't any larger or smaller, and all the unhappy bushes still looked as equally unhappy as they had before.

But something was different. I picked up Sal, closed the door, and leaned against the truck's rear fender.

Maybe the magic looked different. I squinted. The glamour around The Hall had a wave of colors to it—a kind of water-like flow—that wasn't clearly visible on this side, but sometimes I could pick it out.

"What do you think?" I asked my axe.

She mentally inhaled as if breathing in fresh air.

I chuckled. "It does seem cleaner, doesn't it?"

The currents of magical energy around the glamour moved faster, as if the reset had cleared out years' worth of debris from its magical riverbed. Swirls of blue appeared more circular. Woven lines of reds and oranges appeared more evenly braided.

Sal tossed me a distinct sense of *nearby wolf.*

I glanced around. A few of the older wolves could blend into the surroundings so well even I missed them if I wasn't looking. It wasn't magic. They were so good at being wolves that even in human form, they could stalk and ambush prey.

In some ways, the werewolves were more like Benta's cougars than real wolves.

Remy Geroux leaned against the passenger side of his own truck, deep in a shadow and framed more by the lot's bordering stand of trees than his vehicle. He waved and walked over when I noticed him.

"Don't teach your nephew to do that," I said. We didn't need Jax getting into his head that sneaking in and out of Akeyla's room was a good idea.

Remy laughed and slapped my arm. "He'll learn anyway."

"True," I said. Not a lot any of us could do about it.

Remy was slightly smaller than his brother, and stood about the same height as Maura. He was the classic "Special Ops" body type that handled turning werewolf well—lean, fast, and mobile, with a surprising amount of physical strength. Remy, like his brother, could flip a car if he needed to, and it wasn't just his wolf, either. They'd both been stronger than usual before they were bitten centuries ago.

Remy watched the world through hazel, honey-colored irises, which, like his strength, were his and not a byproduct of his wolf, though his eyes did shout "magical creature." I'd long wondered if of the two Geroux brothers, Remy had been the one truly destined for wolf-dom, and not Gerard.

But he wasn't the pack's lead Alpha. His brother and sister-in-law governed better. It never seemed to bother Remy.

"Hello to your axe," he said, and nodded toward Sal's blade.

Sal didn't respond. Either she chose to ignore him, or something about wolf magic didn't blend with her magic, much like the Odin's Gallows dagger and Rose's notebook.

Remy shrugged. "She is not the only elven weapon to ignore me."

"Don't feel bad," I said. "She won't talk to half the elves, either."

He pointed at the glamour. "Something feels different," he said. "For the life of me I cannot pick it out."

"The energy flow around the edges is smoother, and more... geometrically sound." I twirled my finger though the air. "The natural magic there..." I pointed again. "... and there..." Another point. "... looks truer to its spellwork shape."

"I do wish I had your magic-seeing ability," he said.

"The circles and lines that make up the sigils appear more circular and straight."

He nodded. "So they defragged the system?"

I hadn't thought of it that way. "Yeah."

He patted my truck. "I'm here to report on outliers." He nodded toward the town. "We have Mark Ellis in isolation just to be sure. He seems good. No residual vampire enthrallings. Axlam is more concerned about psychological trauma."

The poor kid would be as scarred by the vampires as I was. At least I hadn't been possessed.

Remy leaned closer. "Turns out the two families in town I've long suspected were touched are, in fact, touched."

Arne had been correct—with seven thousand mundanes in the area, someone was likely carrying residual magic the cleansing spells would upset.

"They're okay?"

"Arne will talk to them." Remy walked toward the glamour. "He is the All-Father, after all." He walked to the edge of the lot and the location of the outer gate into The Hall—and stopped. "Shouldn't you be sleeping off the whole mess?"

On my shoulder, Sal *humphed*.

Remy shrugged, then waved his hand. Nothing happened. He waved again.

"I think the reset removed the outer gate," I said.

Remy stuck his hands into his back pocket. "Better for wolves to enter through the doors, anyway." He walked toward the hotel's "entrance."

Most of the wolves left their clothes in the "lobby" before entering The Great Hall. It cut down on naked exits.

I followed Remy toward the doors. "What are you going to do if the coatroom's gone?"

He turned around, threw his arms into the air … and walked backward into the first set of sliding glass doors leading into the hotel lobby.

He turned around. They still did not open.

I walked up. They wouldn't open for me, either. The Great Hall would not allow us in.

"Okay, then," Remy said.

I peered through the glass as if the image inside was truly what we'd walk into if the doors would let us. No unorganized magic. No strangeness. Just a "set to factory default" glamour of the standard interior doors and the lobby beyond.

"How unfriendly." Remy rubbed the side of his nose. "Arne's probably in there getting his ears in a twist because his pack and his paladin haven't yet come to his side."

"They *have* to know we're locked out," I said. We couldn't call. The Hall didn't have cell coverage. We'd have to wait for an elf to come out.

Remy shook his head. "The last time they reset the glamour, they remembered to key us in."

What would distract Arne Odinsson enough that he would forget to allow the non-elf magicals—and me—into The Hall?

Or what would stop him from allowing us in?

"Remy," I said. "Magnus sent a plane down to The Cities, didn't he?"

He shook his head. "I haven't heard."

The doors parted and a gust of "hotel airlock air" rolled out over the concrete entrance walkway were Remy and I stood. Hotel music followed. The reset had upped the quality of the interior glamour.

Two elves I did not recognize walked side by side through the inside set of sliding doors. They glamoured as they passed over the first threshold into two unassuming, if tall, men.

I looked at Remy. He looked at me.

The two elves walked through the outer doors and stopped just outside the entrance. Both took up guard positions.

They were either actual twins, or had figured out how to duplicate their glamours. They were tall even for elves and no more than four or so inches shorter than me. Both glamoured up short-cut nondescript brown hair. Both wore black leather bomber jackets and black sunglasses, and stood like off-duty police or a security detail.

They even carried earpieces.

The one on the left barked what had to be an order. The one on the right echoed his companion.

Traditional elven customs said that when visiting an enclave, one should speak the host's language.

These two weren't speaking English. No, they were speaking the last language I wanted to hear from any elf—Russian.

"You two are Siberians, aren't you?" I asked.

Neither answered.

Remy pointed his thumb at the two elves. "I guess our friends here answer your question about who flew in last night."

I would have expected Icelandic elves—which these two might still be, even though they spoke Russian. The Siberians did farm out their elves as bodyguards.

I shifted Sal to my other shoulder. "We need to speak to either Arne Odinsson or Dagrun Tyrsdottir," I said.

The two elves looked at each other. The one on the left barked out more commands, though they seemed to have slipped from Russian into Icelandic, or perhaps Old Norse.

The two elves stepped together and completely blocked the entrance.

Sal blasted off a wave of *not impressed* and the elf on the right twisted his head slightly as if listening. The one on the left did not.

"My axe wishes to converse with Alfheim's elder elves," I said.

The two shook their heads in unison.

Remy pointed at Sal. "He is the chosen carrier of an elven weapon. Let us in."

They shook their heads again.

Remy pinched the bridge of his nose. He pulled out his phone. After a moment, he spoke into the receiver. "It's Remy. Frank and I stopped by but the two *Taken* wannabees out front won't let us in."

The elf on the right's lip twitched.

"So I'm leaving you this message instead." He hung up. "Arne will call when he has a chance," he said. "Let's go."

"I was there." I stepped forward and stood directly in front of the two elves. "I was in the center of the vampires' spells. I suffered the twisting of my protection enchantments and a blood-draining pike through my heart." I thumped my chest. "What happened was not Arne Odinsson's fault, nor was it the fault of any of Alfheim's elves." I made of point of looking down at the two elves. "Allow us to pass."

Mr. Right inhaled sharply.

I dropped Sal into my hand and stared at Mr. Left. "You do understand that, right now, both of you are within my physical reach?" I could snatch one and slash the other, if I wanted.

Mr. Left's eyes narrowed.

"I am the jotunn of Alfheim." Intimidating elves was not wise, but something told me that if I really was Arne's paladin, I damned well better play it up.

Mr. Right muttered something.

Mr. Left shook his head. "We have orders," he said.

"Yes. I'm sure," I responded.

They looked at each other, then at me. They both shook their heads once again.

I sighed and threw them my best "you disappoint me" look. Sal tossed out her own wave of disappointment. Mr. Right's lip quivered ever so slightly.

"You and your bosses are not of this enclave. *I* am. And I will defend Alfheim and her elves until my last breath."

Remy grinned. Mr. Left stared out into the lot.

Remy saluted the two guards with a hand gesture that said "I'm watching" more than showed respect. "I would pee on your legs but that would be unfriendly."

Mr. Right muttered again.

Remy made a show of sniffing the air. "*Woof,*" he said, and walked away.

I crossed my arms and stared at the two elves. "Welcome to Alfheim," I said, and followed Remy toward our trucks.

CHAPTER 4

Remy leaned against the rear bumper of my new truck. "That was fun." He pointed at the hotel glamour around The Great Hall. "Which King do you think sent them? They were speaking Russian but my money's still on Bragisson."

Tyr Bragisson, our Queen's father, and the default Elf Emperor. "I suspect you are correct. Those two switched to speaking Icelandic." The other Kings in Siberia and Norway were not likely to pull a fly-in on Arne. Only his father-in-law had the power to treat the New World elves like children.

"Dag can't be happy," Remy said.

Good thing Maura and Akeyla moved back into my place this morning. The farther from elven politics they were right now, the better.

Remy tapped the tailgate. "The only time Bragisson has set foot in the New World was when he presented his daughter to our King." He shook his head.

I walked around to the passenger side and set Sal on the seat. Remy followed and leaned against the side panel. "Nice truck, by the way," he said.

"Magnus gifted it to me because the vampires totaled my old one."

Remy looked impressed. "I'll remember that the next time I get in an accident."

I chuckled. "I doubt the vampire excuse will work twice."

He laughed and patted Bloodyhood's rich, wine-colored finish. "After what they put you through, you deserve a fleet, my friend."

I looked back at The Great Hall. The two guards had retreated inside and were no longer visible. Reset magic danced and streamed around the edges of the glamour. Most of the town got through the ordeal intact and okay.

Did I? I wasn't yet sure. Benta assured me that the magicks left no physical wounds. I just...

I closed my eyes. I just didn't want any more unwanted outside forces messing with my home while I recovered.

Remy patted my arm. "I think you should finish resting." He nodded toward The Great Hall. "We both know Arne will put the little Emperor in his place."

Maybe, I thought. Part of me knew that even though the vampires had been dealt with, the situation as a whole had not. And unfinished situations were the only reason guards—and presumably an emissary—from the Icelandic Court would fly to Minnesota.

Arne Odinsson had some explaining to do.

The other elves wanted to know why the Elf King of Alfheim had allowed vampires access to his territory—and also allowed me to live here as well, since I was what drew out Dracula in the first place.

No wonder they wouldn't allow us in.

Remy pulled out his phone. "Not a lot we can do right now, anyway." He walked toward his truck, but looked back at me. "Arne will call," he said, then waved once as he put his phone to his ear.

From inside my truck, Sal agreed. Arne Odinsson was not an elf who backed down. We were probably lucky right now not to be in the middle of the fight.

Though Sal would like to engage in a little swinging and hitting.

I walked around to the driver's side and got in my truck. A new fight was something I'd like to avoid. "Perhaps I need to find you a new itchin'-for-a-battle partner?" I asked my axe.

A wave of ironic *you disappoint me* rolled off Sal. I laughed, though I couldn't help but notice the increase in her conversational skills— and was met with a clear *I chose you.*

"Thank you," I said, and started my truck.

Who knew an axe could be such a good friend?

I TUCKED Sal into the magazine pocket on the back of the passenger seat and made my way into Alfheim's main grocery store. Her handle stuck out between the seats and was visible from outside the vehicle, but around here no one was going to break into my truck anyway, so I figured she was safe.

I loaded up with "magic burger"-worthy ground chuck, fresh potatoes for fries, a new bag of Akeyla's favorite apples, salad greens, a cantaloupe, and a handful of clean-scented, locally-grown tomatoes.

The morning air still held a crispness and the sky gleamed a gorgeous, bright fall blue. Downtown Alfheim gleamed too, as if the reset had washed the grit off the streets. Perhaps it had. Or perhaps I was simply happy to be in The Land of the Living.

Outside town, the trees did a fine job of shading the road, but it'd be nice to get my sunglasses back. They were in the glove compartment of my old truck. I'd call Ed, or Gullinbursti's, tomorrow, and get them back.

I saw the woman with the bicycle as I turned onto the road toward home. The bike's green paint blended into the grass and underbrush, but its rounded, old-style frame and two big saddle baskets behind the seat set it apart.

The back tire had completely deflated, and the woman tugged the bike along the shoulder of the road toward the lake.

I didn't recognize her. She was probably a new neighbor from one of the lake lots, or a tourist from a local lodge. Either way, the truck had plenty of room. I pulled off ahead—plenty ahead, so as not to be frightening—and hopped out.

"Hi!" I called. "I live up the road. Do you need a ride?"

She stopped walking. She stood perfectly still and stared, her lovely rich, auburn hair shimmering in the sunlight and her equally lovely hands on the bike's handlebars.

She was the most beautiful woman I'd ever seen in my entire two centuries. I hadn't noticed when I drove by—I'd been looking at the bike. But I noticed now. Perfect breasts. Perfect hips. A face that even from twenty feet away I knew was just as perfect as the rest of her. Natural, shimmering magic fluttered around her shoulders and arms. Not controlled, wielded magic like an elf or a witch, but soft, gentle magic that mirrored her soft, curved body.

Elves were preternaturally exquisite—they were adjacent to beautiful, and in a lane all their own, like leopards or tigers. They were elves, not humans, and had to be appreciated for their nature.

Real, human beauty was something special.

The woman's lips thinned and she tipped her head as she watched me notice her. I swear she was about to burst into tears.

"Are you okay?" I walked toward her. "My phone's in the truck. I can call someone if you need help." I pointed over my shoulder.

When I looked back, she was wiping her eye. She shouldn't be crying. Not her, because...

I *did* know her. I didn't recognize her, or remember her name, but I knew deep in my bones that we'd talked sometime in the recent past. I'd seen her smile.

"Have we met?" I reached out but realized I was being forward and stuffed my hand into my pocket. We must have met in a particular context, one completely different from this one, and the road must have been interfering with my recollection. "Do you work in town?" Maybe the last time we talked, she was in a uniform, or scrubs.

She didn't answer. She wiped at her eyes again.

I wanted to touch her face and pull her close and stop whatever caused those tears because the deep parts of my soul were roaring *protect*.

"Frank," she said.

She knew my name. I was the idiot with no memories of how we met but *she* knew *me*.

The need to protect almost burst free, but I caught myself and stopped about five feet away. I wouldn't be forward and frightening.

I rubbed the top of my head. "I'm sorry. I don't remember your name."

"That's because you were with that elf this morning," she said.

She knew about Benta being at my place? Her words felt like a slap —like an accusation, as if Benta's presence had been what caused the pain so obvious in the set of her shoulders and the tightness of her hands on the bike's handlebars.

"Marcus Aurelius is at my cottage. I made him stay because I need supplies and didn't want to go into town with your dog." She looked at the trees. "I didn't want to answer questions from the non-magical locals."

"You have my dog?" She'd been looking after my missing hound?

"You sent him with me." She rubbed at her eye again. "I can't do this, Frank. Please go away."

I've been dumbfounded to speechlessness before. At two centuries old, *not* having been dumbfounded into silence would show a significant lack of worldly awareness. But this was the first time I'd been dumbfounded into thoughtlessness.

Nothing swirled in my head. Nothing but the clear, piercing brightness of adrenaline fueled by a genuine, personal, gut-cinching fear that I'd caused this woman pain.

"I can't wake up every morning wondering if I'm going to come down the path to your door and find Benta in your bed. I can't explain to you every goddamned day why you don't remember me. I can't. I can't put you through that. I can't put *me* through that."

She steered the bike to walk around me. "How often do you go into town? Will it always be in that truck, now? I need to know so I can avoid this." She waved her hand between us.

"I don't understand." What else could I say? I had no idea what was happening here.

"No, you don't," she said. "The concealment enchantments wipe your memory every evening." She sniffled. "I'll send Marcus Aurelius home."

"Don't." I *knew* he needed to stay with her. She needed to be safe.

I touched her elbow. "If you're enchanted, I can help. The elves can—"

"No they can't, Frank!" she yelled. "They can't *see* me!" She pushed by. "You will *always* forget me. Always. It doesn't matter how you feel about me or how I…" She stopped and looked up at the sky. "I should have known better. I should have sent you away the moment you walked out of the trees and down to the lakeshore."

I'm not impulsive. I've learned to keep myself under control. I'm measured. Determined. But my need for her came out of nowhere, burst through my chest as if my brother's pike had done its job and now my unfounded emotions for a woman I did not remember bled from my heart. My soul dripped onto the ground.

Because of concealments and enchantments. Because someone wanted me to forget and for her to be hidden. "Don't go," I said. "Tell me what I need to know. What I need to do to help. Please."

She turned her back to me, but didn't walk away. She stood next to the road holding her broken bicycle as she tried not to cry. "My name is Ellie," she said. She glanced over her shoulder.

I extended my hand. "Frank Victorsson," Maybe I could fix this. "It's nice to meet you again, Ellie Jones."

She turned around. Her eyes and her mouth—her entire face —rounded.

Ellie Jones. She'd come down the path and she hadn't run away from my cold morning touch. I hadn't remembered then, either. "Ellie," I whispered.

She dropped the bike and extended her arms.

I had one moment, one memory back—and I *had* hurt her. Not intentionally. Not in a planned way.

Two strides and I picked her up because I had to fix this. I had to. Right there on the side of the road, I scooped my arm under her bottom and lifted her into the air so her chin was level with my mouth.

She wrapped her arms around my neck and pressed her forehead against my temple. Her breath tickled my cheek, and the warmth of her body eased my aches—the small pains, the pricks and kinks—the inner echoes in my bones because loneliness makes me hollow.

I learned to live with the pain long, long ago. I am not easy for a woman to love. Not with the frightening size, scars, and lumbering, physical or otherwise. But Ellie Jones kissed the bridge of my nose and none of the horrors my father baked into my body mattered. She kissed my lips and all my mistakes fell away.

I needed to remember her. I needed *her*.

Some memories filtered back into my mind. Ellie ran away when she realized Benta had stayed last night.

"I'm sorry," I said. Ellie curled around me without reservations or distaste for my skin. "I'm sorry. It'll never happen again." I kissed her chin and her jaw. "I swear. I am so sorry."

Ellie shook. A sob broke through and she pressed her face against my neck, but she held on.

Spells, enchantments, magical gearwork, vampires—I should have remembered anyway. Deep down inside, I should have realized. "I'll figure out what needs fixing. I promise."

She let go. Her arms came off my neck and she pushed on my shoulders until I set her down. "Then what?" She stepped back.

"Ellie." I reached for her again. Her touches, her sobs swirled around my head like a dream. We lacked a past and a future. All we had was this disconnected present moment.

All I had was this thin faith that what I did not remember had been true and good. That all my subsurface emotions erupted because my soul knew what my mind did not.

And now Ellie backed away.

"We'll make it work," I said. A cliché, yes, but the truth.

She shook her head. "What happens when magic moves my world again? After you figure out what needs fixing and *poof* I vanish forever anyway, Frank?" She held out her hand. "It *will* happen. My mother's magic will realize I have connections here and it'll move me. I'm going to vanish one day. I can't do that to you. I can't."

Her foot slid back. "I'm sorry I wrapped you up in my life."

"Ellie." I reached for her again.

All sense of possibility left her face. Every belief and hope. It all vanished into a mask that screamed *I give up*.

Ellie Jones ran into the trees.

"Ellie!" I yelled, but she vanished between two trunks and I couldn't follow. I didn't know where to go, or how to find her.

I was alone at the tree line, my truck, her bicycle, and the road behind me, and the empty expanse of trunks, leaves, and undergrowth in front.

Did I imagine her? No, her bike lay on the gravel. Where did she go? I rubbed my head. What kind of concealment enchantments did she suffer?

All the hollowness, all the internal pulls and pinches of my patchwork body screamed. Pain resurfaced. Pain I'd learned to calm and control. Pain that reminded me that I was a singular creature alone in this world. A man without true family or a mate.

I bellowed at the sky.

What else could I do?

CHAPTER 5

Akeyla burst through the door when I pulled up. "Uncle Frank!" she yelled. "Did you get the groceries?" She jumped up and down next to my truck's door. "Mommy texted you because we need oatmeal for cookies."

I did my best to smile. "I didn't see it, honey."

She frowned. "Oh."

"We can make cookies some other time, okay?" I handed her the bag of apples.

Her frown turned into a tight-lipped look of concern. "Why are you sad, Uncle Frank?"

I looked down at my little elven niece. She watched my face as if every single push and pull of my cheeks and jaw put on a puppet show just for her.

Why could women read me so well?

"It's nothing, sweetie," I said. "Take the bag into the house." I nodded at the door just as Jax walked out.

The kid stopped halfway to the truck and sniffed the air as if he smelled everything Akeyla saw in my expressions.

Jax frowned also, but in more of a confused way. Then he jumped up onto the truck's rear fender and leaned over the tailgate. "You found a bike," he said.

"You did?" Akeyla set the bag of apples on the ground and also jumped up onto the bumper. "It's green!" she said.

"Get down," I said. "Both of you." The bike wasn't for them. Why, I couldn't remember. I wanted to remember. I *had* to remember, but no matter how I concentrated, my mind suggested the bike *was* for them. Why else would I have it other than for the kids?

No other explanation made sense.

I slapped the side of the truck.

Akeyla yipped. Jax jumped down. He watched me the entire time he helped Akeyla off the bumper. She pouted but picked up the apples and walked toward the door.

Jax held out his hand for a bag. He didn't say anything, just held out his arm, and waited.

I handed him the meat. He took the bag, looked inside, then walked toward the house.

Maura watched me from the threshold. Her natural magic jumped and flickered, and she crossed her arms.

She moved aside for the kids. "Make sure what needs to go into the fridge gets in, please," she said as Jax passed by.

He nodded and made his way toward the kitchen.

Maura walked out onto the driveway. "What's up, Frank," she said.

I pulled the last bag out from behind the seats and handed it to Maura. "I need to carry Sal," I said.

My axe seemed as distressed by the roadside encounter as I was, partly because Sal was sure someone enchanted had interacted with me, and partly because that interaction had left me upset enough I'd refused to talk to her on the drive to the house.

And now I was having problems remembering what the entire encounter had been about.

Maura pointed at Sal. "Why is the axe angry?"

I set Sal on my shoulder. "Leave it." I couldn't talk about it because Maura was an elf. I couldn't remember, for the same reason. I couldn't ask for help or an opinion. Not that I'd remember to do so soon enough, anyway.

There'd been a woman. I'd already forgotten the color of her eyes.

"I will not *leave it*, Frank. Something obviously happened. You yelled at the kids." She pointed into the house. "You never yell at the kids."

"I did not yell at the kids." I hit the lock button on my truck's key fob and a shrill *beep-beep* echoed between the house and the garage.

"You found a bike you wouldn't let them look at." She walked around to the back of the truck, the groceries in her arms, and peered into the back. Her brow crinkled and she shook her head as if confused.

I couldn't remember the color of *Ellie's* eyes.

Maura stepped back. "Is this a leftover effect from the vampires?"

"Leave it!" I thundered. *Leave me alone*, I thought.

I swung Sal at the sidewall of my new truck between the rear tire and the tailgate. Swung her like a baseball bat right at the brand-new sparkly finish of yet another extraordinary elven gift.

Sal hollered. Magic blasted from her blade. And somehow, my axe stopped herself just before she made contact with the truck.

The shock of hitting the magical equivalent of a concrete wall slammed into my wrists and rocketed up my arms. The force hit my shoulders and my spine, and I staggered back.

"Frank!" Maura yelled. "What's wrong?"

"Leave me alone," I said.

I couldn't remember the color of Ellie's eyes.

"Frank…"

"Maura, leave me alone." I set Sal on the corner of the truck and walked away.

"Frank!" Maura yelled.

I ignored her and pushed through the broken gate. Sunlight hit a bottle and a shimmering spot of green danced across my house's damaged siding. It wiggled and spun much like an elf's natural magic.

Ellie had a natural magic about her, but I couldn't remember that, either.

I would never see her again—no, I would. Her cottage was here, somewhere. I'd see her in town, or walking by the lake. But I wouldn't remember not remembering her, or her kiss, or her arms around my neck. Or all the other moments I know we spent together but had already been erased.

I punched the house. The siding cracked next to the stain left when my brother attacked Arne into yet another crater in my life. I walked to the lake, and dropped down onto the slippery rocks.

Maybe, if I concentrated, I'd remember something. Maybe, this once, not all of Ellie Jones would slip away.

Water lapped at my foot. Insects buzzed. Across the lake, repairs on the Carlson house had begun. And I still could not remember the color of Ellie's eyes.

I might as well get used to it.

THE SUN DROPPED below the trees and spread golds and oranges over the lake. Frogs chirped and the snake Marcus Aurelius liked to chase rustled through the weeds along the deck. I moved off the rocks and up to my sunning mat, but stayed outside.

The kids didn't need to see me waiting out a concealment enchantment. They didn't understand. Neither did Maura. If I was honest, *I* didn't understand. Yet deep in my gut, I knew that when the sun completely vanished, so would my few remaining fractured memories of Ellie.

Akeyla came out to ask me if I wanted a burger. I thanked her and gave her a quick hug, and told her that she and Jax did an excellent job cooking the meal. She kissed my cheek and went back inside.

The glare of headlights arced around the house, and at least two cars pulled into the driveway. Doors slammed, and voices followed.

Axlam had come to pick up Jax. I stayed where I was. Axlam didn't need to see me this way, either.

A male voice floated through the doors and out onto the deck. Arne

Odinsson had escaped the Icelandic elves and made his way to my home—which meant he wanted me for some fight or another. I ignored him and continued to stare at the orange glow the setting sun spread over the water. I was about to lose what little I had left of my Ellie memories. Her auburn hair. Her tears. Her touch. Arne could wait.

The kids came out. Jax laid his hand on my shoulder. He squeezed once with the wisdom only a nine-year-old could have. "Thank you for having me, Mr. Frank." Then he ran to his mother and his car ride home.

Arne stepped out onto the deck. He shut the doors and stood under the darkening sky for close to a full minute. He watched the lake and the Carlson house. He listened to Axlam's car pull away, and Maura and Akeyla cleaning the dishes.

But mostly he watched me ignore him.

He walked down to where I sat cross-legged on my mat.

He folded himself into his own cross-legged, almost serenely yoga-like pose, and inhaled deeply. "Son," he said.

"Arne," I answered.

He looked no different from the last time I'd seen him, when he pushed Dracula's pike out of my chest. His elven ponytail still wiggled behind his head and his magic still wafted around him in great sheets of kingly energy. His ear continued to be as notched as ever, and his scars continued to tell their tales.

His magic shifted and rotated around itself as it always did. Unlike Dag's armor-like gearwork, Arne's magic appeared smoother. Leaner, perhaps. Where Dag was clockwork, Arne's magic had always felt more biological.

Arne Odinsson, warrior king of natural magic.

"Maura said you almost put a hole in Bloodyhood." He nodded toward the house.

I chuckled. "I figured Akeyla would come up with that name on her own." She must have.

Arne grinned. "Sal told me."

"Ah," I said. Of course Sal told her King.

"She also told me she thinks you had another run-in with fae magic."

Seemed Sal had a more consistent memory of Ellie than I did.

"Is this the same magic that you took care of when Magnus brought you out of the vampire's pocket?"

Ellie was in Dracula's shadow land with me? I opened my mouth to answer, but no words come out.

Arne watched my face. His brows cinched, but he nodded as if understanding why I couldn't answer. "Long ago, when I was young, before I took up voyaging with our mundane Norse..." He leaned toward me. "... before I knew that the Mediterranean existed, much less Iceland, Greenland, or Vinland, I knew a fae."

"Is this the evil fae on Gotland? The one who enthralled the hive of low-demons?"

He shook his head. "Oh, no. This fae was a princess." He looked out over the lake and he smiled, which loosened into a wistful chuckle. "Dagrun is the most extraordinary woman I have ever known," he said. "And I have known many women, elven, mundane, witch, kami, spirit, and all versions in between."

And here I thought Arne and Dag had a marriage based on politics and royal blood, but now I wondered.

"I don't think the fae princess was a woman." He chuckled again. "I think she was *femininity*." He looked up at the sky. "You can't fight that."

"I suppose not," I said.

"The moral, son, is that fae magic is primal. It's neither good nor evil. It is what it is and it will grab ahold of your most alive parts." He patted my shoulder. "The best you can do is ride that wave."

I could follow his metaphor with the obvious—navigating women was like surfing a tsunami. But that was simply an excuse for not working on what needed work. Any man could weave an exaggeration—the fish was *that big*, or I fought off *that many*, or my girlfriend was *that unreasonable*. But sometimes you needed to grow up and take responsibility for the wave you caused.

"Do me a favor," I said.

"Anything."

"Help me to remember that I can't be with Benta." She had something to do with why I was sitting here at the foot of my deck watching the lake with a belly full of anger and a head full of haze.

Not that Benta was to blame; my choices when it came to interacting with her were the problem, not her. But I had to start somewhere, and cutting off that dragon's head before it breathed more fire seemed the best course of action.

Arne nodded. "I will, son."

We sat in silence as we watched the rising moon. Arne had come to speak to me about something other than my unintentional attempt to damage my new truck. And me, I was out here because…

… because I'd had a moment on the way home. A twinge that felt as if some horror inflicted by the vampires continued to linger. Because that *had* to be why.

I tapped my chest. "There's nothing left of the spells, is there?" Best to have the Elf King do the checking.

Arne held his hand over my chest. Magic swirled around his fingers and washed from his palm to my breastbone. He shook his head. "You're clean."

So why did I feel as if my heart had shattered?

I looked over my shoulder at the house. Maura shepherded Akeyla toward her bedroom. I rubbed my face. "I found a bike by the road this afternoon. I think I'll fix it up for Akeyla." Someone had run away and left it sitting on the gravel. I should make the best of a bad situation.

"She'll like that," he said. "Feeling better?"

"Yeah." I rubbed at my shoulder. "I think I'm tired. That's all." Why else would I sulk around all morose?

"Good, good," Arne gripped my shoulder again. "Because I need you to pack. I need you to go to Las Vegas."

CHAPTER 6

Dust. Heat. Shallowness and grift. I hated Las Vegas.

Two hundred years of fights both magical and mundane, and the only time I have ever been arrested was in sixty-two, on the Strip, when I punched a conman after his showgirl sidekick swindled me out of three thousand dollars.

I should have known better, but I'd been on a college-and-heartbreak bender and hadn't quite learned yet that not all places in America were like Alfheim.

So Las Vegas was not my favorite city.

"Why?" I asked.

Arne inhaled deeply, and exhaled slowly. "You met the Icelandic emissary guards this morning."

I'd been correct; Tyr Bragisson did pull a fly-in on Arne.

He rubbed his cheek in an exceptionally mundane way. "My father-in-law has called an International Conclave."

"In Las Vegas?" I could think of a thousand better cities than Las Vegas. Hell, Reno would be better. Or Sioux Falls. Or a cornfield in Iowa.

"Tyr Bragisson believes I must explain my inclusive ways not only to him, but to the rest of the Courts." He gestured as if bowing to the night sky. "We are to follow Conclave protocols: No more contact between rulers until we are face-to-face at the Conclave Feast. Parties are to be held to King, Queen, and one elder from each enclave. We're bringing Magnus."

As Alfheim's most charming elf, Magnus was the best choice.

Arne sighed. "I am allowed witnesses." He cocked his head. "Fewer in number than a battle party."

I sniffed. "They do realize who your witnesses will be, right?"

Arne grinned. "My father-in-law killed a witch-turned-werewolf in the Fifteenth Century and now believes he is invincible in the face of all magical threats."

Arne seemed more sad than disdainful, and not at all sarcastic, as if Tyr Bragisson really did feel himself invincible.

"Rules about the early arrival of witnesses are vague," he said. "But such bending will not be looked upon well, so you are to keep a low profile."

"I have never in my two centuries been able to keep a low profile," I said.

"Remy will be with you."

Remy wasn't a low profile kind of person, either.

Arne did not appear concerned. "Protocols decree no glamours during the Conclave Feast. We are not to hide from our equals." He tapped the decking under us. "There is a costume convention in Las Vegas this coming weekend. Tyr's emissary has informed me that such occasions offer cover and plausible deniability for any out-of-glamour encounters."

The Elf Emperor called an International Elven Conclave and was using a fantasy convention as cover. With that many angry, yelling elves around, an out-of-glamour encounter was inevitable, and cover a good idea.

"Here I thought the kami were the practical magicals," I said.

Arne shrugged. "Many of the kami are better at mundane interactions than elves. Or, perhaps, their mundanes are better at interacting with the kami."

37

"Don't sell yourself short, Arne," I said. "You're the elf setting up the New Zealand enclave. Not Tyr and not the kami."

He stared at the Carlson house across the lake. "Some of the kami believe we were born of the rubbing of magic against the mundane. That all the magicals—elves, kami, spirits, fae—are sparks caused by the mundane's grinding off the edges of the natural world." He mimicked the motion of sanding a plank. "Add a little sunshine and you get the good. Add a little darkness, and you get the bad."

Sounded about right. "That's pretty much how it works in The Land of the Dead, with the vampires and the demons," I said. "Except magicals are born of the energy of the living instead of the rage of the dead."

"Aye," Arne said. "I still must explain myself."

He did. Magicals had rules.

"Bragisson's guards seem well-suited to their job," I said.

His lip twisted. Arne stared out over the lake.

"So you found them as annoying as Remy and I did?"

"Beware the *real* Cold War spies." Arne chuckled. "They did not return to Reykjavík with the emissary." He leaned close again. "I suspect you and Remy will not be the only early arrivals."

Las Vegas was going to be crawling with spying "witnesses."

Arne patted my shoulder. "You and Remy are to go tonight. I need you two to find someone. The Feast is scheduled for Thursday evening, the first major day of the costume convention. That will give you four days to search."

"Tonight? I take it Magnus brought in a plane for us."

Arne nodded. "He knows you can't fly unless it's private or first class, and with the urgency and the… nature… of the task, we decided to bring in a charter."

"Who are we looking for?" I asked.

He returned to looking out over the lake at the Carlson house. "Remy will fill you in," he said.

Which was the answer I suspected I'd get, even if it was not the answer I wanted. "Should I bring Sal?" I motioned at the house. "See if

38

Rose's notebook will cough up another dagger made from Odin's Gallows?"

His eyes narrowed and his lips thinned. Arne Odinsson was legitimately considering what I asked.

Great, I thought.

"She's not a vampire, Frank," he said. "Not really."

Great turned into a string of profanity.

He sighed again. "Tony and Ivan weren't the first dark magicals I've taken in."

"I figured as much," I said.

Arne absently picked at my deck. "She lived here a long time ago, before Dagrun came from Iceland. Remy remembers her."

Arne thumped the decking. "Find her. Explain the situation. Ask her if she is willing to step forward as a dark magical and explain to the Courts how she chose to come to neutral after we offered a path."

"Neutral, huh?" He'd held Tony and Ivan at neutral for seventy years, and probably would have for seventy more, if they hadn't been re-tempted to the dark side.

"Compassion will not turn a dark magical into a friend, but it will increase the chances of an alliance against a mutual enemy."

"The enemy of my enemy is my diplomatically aligned trade partner?" No wonder Arne was the elf setting up the new enclave.

He grinned. "Or so they say, my son."

"Why aren't you the Elf Emperor?" But I knew: Arne was King of the only New World enclave and much too far away from the main elf business.

He laughed. "Why would I want to be Emperor and have to deal with yelling Siberians on a daily basis?" He shook his head. "Better we take in more vampires."

The vampires were what got us here in the first place. The vampires and my witch-daughter, Rose. "So this woman we'll be looking for, she's your ace in the hole?" Whoever she was, Arne was hoping her testimony would sway the court, so to speak.

Arne squeezed my shoulder again. "My father-in-law does not believe the success of the Alfheim Pack is correctly illustrative of my ways." He shook his head. "Nor does he see you as anything other than an oddity."

"That's comforting," I said. At least the other Courts didn't think of me, or the wolves for that matter, as dark magicals, though the dismissive attitude irked me.

"I ask that you and Remy speak at the Feast, no matter what the rest of my kind believe."

I nodded. I'd do what I could.

"Good." He looked out over the lake again and shook his head. "My father-in-law agreed to sanction your and Remy's testimonials. I believe he thinks that my witnesses aren't truly dark and that your presence will only serve to reinforce his belief that Alfheim needs a guiding hand."

Remy and I were to find a magical bad enough to look dark in the eyes of the other elven Courts. One who, unlike the pack, was so dark that coming to neutral was the best Arne could do.

I wasn't sure such a witness was a good idea.

Arne looked resigned. "Even if we end up with a full moratorium on witches, vampires, and dark spirits, the other elves need to understand that the world does not end at the gates of their Great Halls."

Arne's magic flared. He'd been calm and collected since he sat down on the deck next to me. Confident and cool and practiced. But his magic just betrayed an internal churning.

"So, Sal or no Sal?" I asked.

He thought about it for a moment. "No weapons at International Conclaves," he said. "No matter how interesting her evolution has been these past few days."

The twins were probably carrying their fair share of mundane weapons, though. "Too bad. I suspect Sal would like a word with Tyr Bragisson."

Arne *humphed.* "She was never so... alive... before." He patted my shoulder. "You're good for her. She's growing."

Whether or not a magical elven battle axe "growing" was good for the world, I did not know, but she was definitely good for me. "So her full name is Salvation? Seems a bit ironic, don't you think?" And odd, since she was an elven weapon. "Shouldn't her name be in Old Norse?"

Arne laughed. "One day, she may tell you her story." He stood with the graceful elegance all the elves shared. Arne might be large and strong—he stood taller and wider than most mundanes—but he still moved like a dancer even when lifting himself off the ground.

"The plane is ready." He nodded toward the house. "Remy will meet you at the airfield. Dagrun, Magnus, and I will join you Thursday at our appointed time." He stretched his shoulders. "Remy got you rooms in the Conclave hotel. None of the Courts will be staying there." He shrugged. "This convention—ElfCon, Remy called it —has booked the entire building."

"The convention is called ElfCon?" The elves would likely be as amused as they were annoyed by the costume choices of the mundanes on hand.

Arne slowly inhaled and exhaled once again, as if attempting to keep his disappointment under control. "Ironic. I know."

"I'll get myself to the airstrip," I said. Looked like no extra rest for me tonight. I'd better get my bag packed.

"You don't have a lot of time," Arne said.

No, we did not. "We may not find her." Unless Remy had good leads, four days often wasn't enough for such an investigation.

"Try. Please."

"We will." Remy and I would do our best. "Thursday, then."

Arne extended his hand to help me up even though I outweighed him by at least one hundred pounds.

I took it. A little stability never hurt.

"With each new day comes a newer and greater responsibility." He clasped my arms. "The Courts will all understand the value of my ways."

I stared down at the elf I considered more of a father than the man who stitched me together. It was Arne who taught me how to live in this world. Arne and Dag taught me how to contain my rage. They gave me the tools I needed to understand that the colors I saw around people were representations of their magic.

41

They taught me how to be whole, and now Arne needed me to find someone who could make the case that such wholesomeness was worthwhile.

I hoped he was correct.

He walked toward the path to the front of the house. "Hug Akeyla for me."

"I will," I said, and made my way inside.

MAURA WAVED as her father pulled his car around and made his way down my driveway. She watched until his taillights vanished into the trees, then turned toward the house.

I watched from the door. Akeyla—teeth brushed but still in her day clothes—hugged my leg.

She yawned. "I don't want to go to bed," she said.

I picked her up. Now that she was almost nine, only Arne and I had the strength to carry her around. Neither of us minded when she asked.

She hugged my neck as she watched her mother return to the house. "Grandpa said you're leaving tonight."

"I am," I said.

"Are you still sad, Uncle Frank?" She snuggled in again.

"I'm better. Your grandpa and I talked."

"Good," she said, and wiggled so I'd put her down. "You don't need to be sad." I obliged just as Maura stepped in and closed the door.

Why I had been "sad," I wasn't quite sure. Arne said I was clean of vamp magic. That didn't mean I was clean of their damage.

Perhaps a couple of days away from Alfheim would set my mind straight, even if that "away" was Las Vegas.

"Go put on your pajamas," Maura said to her daughter.

Akeyla yawned and shuffled off toward her room. Her busy day manifested in her young bones the same way it did for all kids, magical or otherwise—half asleep on her feet but still excited enough to not want to go to bed.

Maura watched her go. "If you need to talk about what happened with the vampires, I'm here. Instead of swinging Sal at your truck, I mean."

Benta had said the same thing. Not about Sal, but about discussing vampiric aftereffects. "I know." I gave her a quick side-by-side hug. "Thanks for moving back in."

Maura poked my side. "Akeyla likes your place. She likes the lake." She nodded toward the back of the house. "I think she likes the calming effect the natural magic here has on her fire spirit."

She looked up at my face. "And she loves her Uncle Frank."

"I love her," I said. "Both of you."

Maura squeezed my hand. "So Dad has you and Remy running recon in Vegas, huh?"

"Looks that way."

"Be careful." She touched my arm again. "We don't have tricksters here in Alfheim. Dad keeps them under control." She shook her head. "He'll bring in vampires and witches and werewolves, but a trickster elf? Nope."

I'd heard rumors about some of the smaller enclaves under Norwegian rule. About how they didn't have the power level necessary to control the worst of their kind.

It got elves killed, International Conclaves called, and kings deposed.

Was Arne sending us to Vegas to scout an elven trickster? Maybe. Maybe not. Either way, Remy would tell me once I reached the airfield.

Maura watched her daughter. "All the magicals have tricksters. Elves, kami, fae, spirits of all kinds, including the New Zealand and Polynesian spirits we're finally building relationships with. Tricksters eat vulnerability for breakfast."

"My vulnerability, or your father's?" I asked.

Maura walked toward Akeyla's room. "Both of you." She winked and stopped in front of the threshold.

"I'll be careful," I said.

She moved her foot across the floor just inside Akeyla's door as if attempting to avoid slipping on something I could not see. "We'll take care of your place while you're gone." She frowned, then blinked as if confused.

"I'll find your dog, too. So don't worry." Her foot kicked a notebook out into the hall. Then Maura Dagsdottir stepped into her daughter's room.

I stared at the notebook. Smiling sherbet-colored unicorns and flying horses danced across the cover.

I picked it up. Maura and Akeyla were fully engaged in their bedtime activities. Something told me that they wouldn't attend to the notebook anyway, even if I did interrupt. I flipped it open.

The first page contained notes, in my blocky hand, about someone named Chihiro Hatanaka, who lived in Tokyo. The next page, notes about a village in Germany. The next, San Francisco. The next held a little sketch of a kangaroo, all obviously written and drawn by me.

When did I take one of Akeyla's notebooks and write international notes? I flipped the book over and checked it for magic.

Nothing. It was simply a third grader's school notebook.

I walked into the kitchen and set the notebook next to a pile of mail. I'd ask Arne when I got back if he thought perhaps the vamps messed with my memory.

Outside, the waning moon shimmered across the lake. Inside, my sister flipped off the lights in my little niece's bedroom and turned on her nightlight. Little stars, unicorns, and happy birds danced across the hallway wall opposite her door.

Even if the vampires did extra damage to me, they were gone, and Akeyla and Maura were safe. And I could handle a trickster or two.

I made my way to my own bedroom to pack my bag.

CHAPTER 7

"She called herself Portia Elizabeth when she lived in Alfheim." Remy tucked his bag under the Cessna's buttery champagne-colored leather seat.

Magnus had booked us one of his charter company's six-seater corporate jets, with a sleek "chrome and ice" interior. The bar glistened as if cut from a glacier, and the thankfully oversized seats swallowed up a body whole.

The plane came with a pair of pilots who held their interactions to "Welcome aboard" and pre-flight checks. No attendant, which didn't surprise me at this time of night. The co-pilot ran through safety information and instructions on how to serve ourselves from the bar.

I tucked my own bag under my seat. "And no one knew what she was?"

Remy tucked his copy of *The Atlantic* into the pocket next to his seat. "The consensus was that she was a spirit. The only thing we knew for sure was that she wasn't indigenous to North America." He sat and fiddled with his seatbelt. "The native spirits were as confounded by her as the elder elves."

Only three times in my life had I met a native North American spirit. One was while I walked the Canadian Arctic into Alfheim. We didn't communicate, but he followed me for a full week. Honestly, looking back, I think he found my hounds fascinating and was protecting them from cougars and bears.

The second was while I walked with Rose north along the Mississippi. That spirit, too, had not interacted, and again looking back, I think she had been more interested in Rose than in me.

The third time I met an indigenous spirit was about fifteen years ago, when Arne began a serious attempt to atone for Alfheim's past with the local communities.

For the most part, the indigenous magical populations of the Americas wanted nothing to do with the elves, fae, and kami, mostly because the non-native magicals always sided with their cultural mundanes. Always, no matter the atrocity.

The elves had more contacts among the Southern Hemisphere Pacific Rim spirits and magicals than they did with the magicals on whose land they lived.

Remy watched me stuff myself into my seat. He half-smirked as if part of his brain found the dance I did to get my huge body comfortable in a seat not built for an almost-seven foot, three-hundred-pound man to be funny. The other part of Remy's face betrayed his empathy for my situation.

But that was Remy. He was a hooligan unless someone needed help, and he often knew before the person in need even realized they needed that help.

He chalked it up to his wolf senses. I chalked it up to him recognizing *everyone* as pack—mundanes, magicals, dogs, cats, horses, it didn't matter. No matter what the international elves thought of werewolves, the world was a better place because the Geroux brothers learned how to live with—and utilize—their curse.

Remy's hooliganism did make him entertaining, though.

The co-pilot closed the door just as the pilot announced that they would have us in Las Vegas in about four hours. Magnus had already given us our rental car and hotel information, and had suggested we sleep, since we'd be arriving in the middle of the night.

"Has Arne ever told you about his fae earth goddess princess?" Remy asked.

"He's mentioned her," I said. Remy must have meant Arne's fae of femininity.

The plane's engine revved, and we began to taxi. The pilots closed their door and turned down the cabin lights.

Remy leaned his head against his seat. "When Portia Elizabeth showed up, I think he thought she was his princess."

The twitches moving across Remy's face said that Arne wasn't the only magical in town who thought Portia Elizabeth was some sort of primal female spirit.

"This was the mid-sixteen hundreds," Remy said. "Gerard and I were just coming to terms with the elves and what they offered, and we were still a bit skittish."

The plane accelerated for take-off.

Remy grinned as he flopped back into his seat. "I will never forget the day she walked into town," he said.

The plane climbed and we both concentrated on popping our ears until we leveled off. The engine roared, but the little jet was quieter than most of the other small planes I'd been in.

"I brought something," Remy said. He pulled his bag out from under his seat and flopped it onto his lap.

The zipper's grinding vanished into the plane's noise, as did the bag's rustling. Remy lifted out a leather satchel about the size of a large manila envelope.

Gentle magic curled around the pouch—gentle magic I recognized. "It's carrying protection spells," I said.

Remy set the pouch on his thigh and stuffed his bag back under his seat. "They're preservation spells." He untied the string holding the flap in place and flipped it open.

The spells didn't change.

"Interesting," I said.

"The spells form a sort of stasis." Remy pulled out a leather bound notebook not unlike Rose's. "Nothing inside ages."

The spells were a lot more intricate and complicated than they looked, then. I peered at the pouch. "I need to get me one of those," I said. "For Rose's notebook."

Remy tapped the pouch. "It's bearskin. The elder elf who made it passed before you came to Alfheim."

Arne or Dag might still find value in enchanting a satchel for Rose's notebook, if for no other reason than to keep an eye on it.

Gently and with reverence, Remy opened the notebook. The first page was full of lovely handwritten French script, as were the next two pages.

The fourth page held a sketch of what looked like the shores of Lake Superior. The fifth a sketch of what appeared to be a Native American encampment. The next few pages were portraits.

"For a while, I was filling one of these a year." A slight smile danced over his lips as he touched the pages. "When I could get my hands on paper and pencil or pen." He looked up. "I still have forty-seven, all of them dating from our acceptance into Alfheim forward."

"Are they all enchanted?" I asked. "Preserved?"

He shrugged. "They are now." He flipped the pages and held up the book so I could see the portrait. "I drew this picture in 1657. This gentleman was the Chief of the Ojibwe band who lived near Alfheim. I wish I remembered his name."

Remy sighed. "I remember his middle daughter." He shook his head. "She spoke fluent French and English, and had a gift for navigation. She was murdered by two English traders. Gerard and I ripped them apart and brought her family their heads."

He shook as if the memory pulled up all of its corresponding anger and shock. "Those were different times."

He flipped to another page and held up the book again. "I don't remember her name, either."

The portrait showed a young woman with worldly eyes, as if she had been studying Remy as much as he had been studying her.

He flipped the book around. After a moment, he flipped through a few more pages. "Here," he said, and held it up again.

The woman in the drawing lifted her skirts so that she could step over a puddle. Her hair was loosely bundled and fell around her shoulders, and she carried a bag.

Honestly, no matter Remy's portraiture skill, she looked unremarkable.

Remy frowned and flipped through a few more pages. He held up the book again. "A closer look at her face."

He'd drawn her hair black, so I assumed she was a brunette of some flavor. Her large eyes also appeared dark, and her lips full. Her features were round yet sharp, and looked Persian. She, like the young woman he showed me earlier, carried a worldly, intelligent expression.

She was beautiful, but not remarkable.

Remy closed the book and slipped it back into its enchanted satchel. "And that, right there, is her superpower."

I frowned. "I don't understand."

"Portia Elizabeth *will* get under your skin. You just won't realize it until you're husband number three living in a cabin outside of town because she wants her favorite in a special place."

"That's awfully specific, Remy," I said.

He returned the book and its enchanted pouch to his bag. "Pretty much *all* I remember from the decade she lived in Alfheim is *her*. Without the notebooks, I probably wouldn't even remember the two traders Gerard and I ripped apart."

He looked out the window. "She asked me to take care of them. She was livid that they'd hurt the Chief's daughter."

"So this Portia Elizabeth has some sort of enthralling ability?" I asked.

"I wouldn't call it *enthralling* so much as *interweaving*. She becomes indispensable to a man's soul. She becomes purpose." He rubbed at the top of his head. "There were three of us—an elf, a mundane, and me. She loved us all, and we all loved her. We didn't fight. We didn't complain. Honestly, none of the men did when she was around. The town functioned better," he said. "Arne was head over heels in love with her, too, but she kept him at arm's length."

"Doesn't sound all that bad," I said, though losing your will and ability to choose for yourself was, even if some people liked that. Some people wanted to hand over all their intra- and interpersonal decisions to someone else. "I'm sure there were plenty who were willing to follow her around."

Remy snorted. "Like a goddess. That was the issue. You know how we're so careful with Magnus? Because if we left him to his own devices, he'd do exactly the same thing. He'd charm every mundane within a hundred miles of Alfheim, not because he's bad, but because he's so damned *good*."

All the elves fit into that category.

"But Portia wasn't *good*. She was *primal*. Primal means a lack of civilization. Primal means dancing and writhing and a lot of sex."

Ah, the crux of the issue.

"I couldn't get enough of her. Neither could any of the other men in town—all the men, by the way. If you had a Y chromosome, no matter your proclivities, she had an effect. She didn't seem to have a lot of effect on the women, at least sexually." He wiggled in his seat. "I don't know if Arne kicked her out or if she left on her own. I think she made the decision to leave. Arne was trying to help her tame her magic. He was trying to teach her how to be less primal and more strategic. He did, at least according to him. But all I remember is that I wasn't myself for at least three years after she left. I was weak, both physically and mentally. Gerard, too. The elves handled it better. It wasn't until Dag and the infusion of new elf blood that came with her that Alfheim fully recovered."

Never had I met such a spirit. Never had Arne or any of the elves warned me, either.

But I was pretty sure I knew what kind of spirit Portia Elizabeth was—and why I wasn't surprised she'd chosen Sin City as her base of operations.

Stars and clouds drifted by outside. Under us, dots glimmered like islands in the pitch black. Not many cities filled the plains between Minneapolis and Las Vegas.

"Remy," I said.

He looked up as he pulled out a blanket from the pocket next to his seat.

"We're going to Vegas to look for a succubus, aren't we?"

He tucked a pillow against the side of his seat and leaned back. "Yes," he said. "Yes, we are."

CHAPTER 8

A lot of primal spirits were demonized in the early Christian days of the Roman Empire. Lots of the world's magical ecology was wiped away by the howling onslaught that was hurricanes Constantine and Justinian. Such is the way of fearful, powerful men.

Not a lot has changed.

So I suspected that the spirit who called herself Portia Elizabeth wasn't the man-eater the label "succubus" suggested. I just didn't know what else to call her.

But that didn't diminish the danger she presented to those who did not understand who and what she embodied. Not that I understood, but at least I knew what I was getting myself into, and knowing what you are walking into is half the battle.

The plane taxied to the charter terminal and our pilots increased the lights enough that we could disembark. They thanked us both, and we stepped off the little Cessna into the nighttime, desert air.

Too much dry, dusty heat hit me full in the face.

Night in the desert carried a different kind of predatory ambiance than in northern climates. Here, no trees hid monsters. No lakes or rivers or streams blocked a frontal attack.

Here, only the shadows stood between you and the stalking beasts.

We were deep enough into autumn that the night temperatures had dropped to brisk, but the air still desiccated my lungs as if someone had stuffed me full of silica packets.

Remy, though, didn't seem to mind. Remy seemed right at home.

He stretched and yawned, and sniffed at the cool night air. "Jet fuel." He leaned his head to the side and sniffed again. "Insomnia." He leaned the other way. "And the Placebo Effect."

I shook my head.

Remy threw wide his arms and walked backward toward the bright lights of the terminal. "Happiness is a drug, my friend, and Vegas is the biggest medicinal lie there is."

I laughed. So under it all, Remy didn't like Vegas any more than I did.

He touched his nose before turning around. "The desert is the true drug," he called over his shoulder.

We checked through the terminal and made our way to our waiting rental. I wanted to settle into our hotel on the Strip and sleep. Remy had other plans.

None of his online searches had pulled up anything or anyone who might be our target, but he still had leads. "Mark didn't remember the address specifics of the apartments," he said.

Mark Ellis, the wolf molested by the vampires, had spent about a year or so as a transient before Gerard and Remy found him. Most of that time had been in the Southwest.

Somewhere in the city, magicals lived in an apartment complex. Mark remembered talk while there of a "woman in red" who could have been a succubus.

Mark figured the apartments had some sort of low-level concealment enchantment that made remembering specifics difficult.

Remy figured I'd see the magic around the building even with a low-level enchantment.

We find the apartments. We ask questions. And hopefully, we find Portia Elizabeth.

"We have four days," he said as he tossed his bag into the back of the rental SUV. "We start now."

Four days to find one spirit in a city of three million people. "What's the magical population here?" I asked.

The SUV dinged as he inserted the key. "There's no permanent enclave of elves or kami, if that's what you're asking. This place is too transient for any of the magicals to take root." Remy smoothed the front of his dress shirt.

The kami had North American enclaves in San Francisco, Seattle, Vancouver, and New York City. Their largest and most powerful New World enclave operated in Peru, and tended toward "unseemly behavior," according to the elves. I never asked for specifics. But the kami were generally better at the complexities—seemly and unseemly alike —than any of the other magicals, except the wolves and elves of Alfheim.

So a small kami enclave in Las Vegas seemed possible. But without permanent magical residents, we would most likely be talking to mundanes. And at this time of the night, mundanes liked to talk, and any little help we could muster to find our target, the better.

Night magic, Rose used to call it, and it was utterly of the mundanes. At night, they were prey, and nothing makes prey huddle more than the threat of unseen predators.

Remy was both predator and protector. He confused the magic and opened up the souls of the afraid.

We slid past the rental yard's gates and into the Las Vegas night.

The Strip never shut down. The hotels and casinos never closed. The lights stayed on and the money rolled, but the desert always nipped at the shores of the mundanes' island of fantasy.

The desert magic, though, felt less hospitable than Alfheim, as if it understood that Las Vegas wasn't a simple buoy. Vegas was a drilling platform in the middle of pristine waters and the ocean here was not happy about its presence.

Remy understood. He might be more protector than predator, but his hackles were up, and his concentration keen on the dark streets flowing by outside the SUV.

Remy's nose wrinkled. "Don't you smell it?" he asked. "The transience?"

The last time I set foot in Vegas, you needed to go outside to travel the Strip. Now, the hotels were all intertwined inside a net of shopping-mall-like hallways and restaurant-lined tunnels. Once you entered, you literally did not need to step outside into the heat unless you wanted to visit "old Vegas" or take a daytrip into the desert.

Nothing about the setup felt cozy. Or transient. It felt like an inescapable trap.

"Not so much smell as see," I said.

Remy stopped for a light. The stoplights hung on their poles and the desert crept in on the heat wafting off the still-hot pavement. Up ahead, the unending glow of the Strip still could not fight back the blackness of the night sky.

"You see magic here?" Remy asked.

I hadn't really looked. Every location had a natural magic. Plants, animals, mundanes and magicals—they produced currents. And currents meant energy, but cities had a technological energy that swamped any- and everything natural.

We were a few blocks off the Strip. The houses here were "vintage." The concrete, old and cracked by decades of desert sun. This part of Las Vegas had a griminess—but not dirt. Dust blew in—some parts of nature would not be deterred—and the constant blasting stripped paint and patina alike.

Or perhaps the mundanes here had been stripped of their faces and facades.

Maybe, perhaps, places like this were where the mundanes rubbed up against magic. Maybe people made wishes in these forgotten corners of humanity. Perhaps here was where magicals were born.

I shook my head and frowned. I must have been more exhausted than I thought.

"Maybe," I said. Was I looking at magic?

Most of the ambient magic floating between the walled yards and deserted convenience stores mimicked the golds and greens of the glitz and glimmer rising over the Strip. It carried right angles. It stopped and started. But it also pulled and coiled in ways that suggested that whatever they'd paved over to build the hotels had been powerful indeed.

My gut said that deep underground, there was a primordial importance here. There were also people. The waves of magic around me supported my instincts. But honestly, I knew nothing of this place beyond my own distaste.

"I'm not sure what I'm looking at," I said.

Remy sniffed again. "And that, I believe, is the core of Las Vegas." He straightened his cuffs as he looked up at my face. "This place is a glamour."

Perhaps. Though my gut said *glamour* wasn't quite the correct descriptor.

"Watch for magicals and mundanes who understand what we are." He turned left onto one of the major streets leading to the Strip. "Someone might know something."

Every road in Las Vegas led to the Strip. Every corner, every path. Everything led to the pillar of light cutting through the terror of the night.

Beyond the horizon, out on the edge of the world, the cherry-red glow of the approaching dawn ever-so-slightly backlit the mountains.

We were about to lose the night magic. I peered at the smaller, older hotels and casinos rising up along the edges of Las Vegas's wonderland.

There had to be someone here, somewhere.

"There." I pointed at a boardwalk overhang of one of the smaller, older casinos. The lights blared, but the gates were still closed even though the sign proudly advertised "24 hours of gaming."

A trail of craggy magic drifted through the casino's one open entrance.

Whoever this magical was, he or she wasn't particularly good at full glamours.

Remy pulled up front and rolled down the windows. He sniffed. "*Hmmm...*" he said. The wolves could scent out just about anything. "I do believe you are correct."

We parked. As we walked toward the entrance, Remy adjusted the cufflinks he'd put in before we exited the plane. He'd decided to play "rich, magical high roller" for the evening and that the cufflinks would be enough to transform his travel white shirt and black slacks into a persona that garnered respect. I, in my jeans and t-shirt, was to be his de facto bodyguard.

Ornate, intricate chandeliers hung from the ceiling and added a hint of deadly nature to the casino floor. Lights behind the glass oscillated and the entire structure rotated through a brittle rainbow of dangerous stalactites.

A hint of lovely danger never hurt to get the blood pumping and the money flowing.

Slot machines dinged. Dealers called out cards. The roulette table jangled and jingled, and the three drunken old men pushed chips toward their chosen color.

The shadows between the banks of slots thickened into coarse points of darkness that, to my magic-seeing eyes, looked as if they had a prickly texture.

A bored, dark-haired woman with no obvious magic wiped at a glass behind the bar and watched us walk across the casino floor. She didn't give us any more attention than she gave the drunk at the end of the bar.

One older lady with her cup of fake gold casino coins looked up at us. Her eyes narrowed—and the magic around her puckered.

Troll, I thought. A real troll. The dangerous kind who stayed away from humans. They tended to fixate on specific locations—mountains, hills, boulders, and bridges—and never left unless driven out.

Remy grinned. "Well, well," he said, and walked toward her slot machine. "Look what we have here."

Her glamour reflected the disparity between her visible size and what the air currents around her suggested. She was hunched, and condensed, but gave off a clear air of appearing smaller than she truly was.

Her gray hair gave off a granite-purple cast even in the golden casino light, as if, as a troll, she had already made her peace with her eventual turning to stone. The wrinkles of her face lacked a true three-dimensionality, as if she didn't quite understand how to glamour properly.

The screen on her slot machine screamed through images and colors, and cast a sulfur-fire glow onto her loose old-lady polyester and her gaudy, gold jewelry.

She curled her hand over her big cup of coins and hissed at Remy. "Wolf," she spat out.

Remy extended his hand. "Remy Geroux," he said. "Alfheim Pack Alpha."

She clutched the cup to her chest and sunk into the padding of her chair. "You live with *elves*," she spat out in a clipped, Danish accent. She looked me up and down. "What are *you*?"

"I'm a jotunn," I said.

She slapped her leg. A loud, chortling cackle followed, and she pointed a finger at my chest. "Do not let real jotnar hear you say that, boy!"

I glanced at Remy. He shrugged. "Real jotnar" were not likely to show up any time soon. Or at least that was what Arne claimed.

The troll continued to cackle. "So many of you in my space," she coughed out.

"I thought trolls stayed away from mundanes," Remy said.

She sniffed and held out her hand. "Vacation for the arthritis." She shook her head as if Remy was the dumbest wolf she'd ever encountered. "Too many tourists visit my rocks, now. The warm is better."

"Casinos aren't exactly natural," I said.

She pointed at the floor. "Still land." She pointed upward. "Still mountain." Then swirled her finger at the chandelier-encrusted ceiling. "Still cave."

"Still gold." Remy pointed at her cup.

Trolls had the same variety of attributes among their kind that the wolves, vampires, and all magicals other than the elves did—if there was a story, that particular type of troll walked the Earth somewhere.

This one liked gold more than she detested humans.

She rubbed at her cheek. "You still *wolf*." She forced the final 'f' sound out between her lips as if she was a deflating tire.

Remy leaned over so they were eye-to-eye. "There's a place here. An apartment complex. One of my wolves stayed there not too long ago. We need to find it," he said.

The troll's lips thinned. She clearly knew of the place. "Why would I care where the locals live?" she said.

"We're looking for someone," Remy said.

The troll frowned. "Of course you are. You be the big bad *wolf.*" She deflated the 'f' again. "Your kind gets fixated."

"Fixated? This from a troll," Remy said.

She sniffed at him again. "You an *old* wolf. Old wolves not trustworthy."

Remy rolled his eyes. "A woman. A spirit. Affects men." Remy's cheek twitched.

"Oh! You stalking, wolfie? *Woof woof.*" She swirled her finger again. "The mundanes have laws now, you know."

Remy simply stared at her. No blinking. No pinching the bridge of his nose. Only a silent, still, pointed glare directly at her eyes.

She looked away. "Lots of women here affect men."

"How many?" I asked. Were succubi common? I had no idea.

The troll pointed at Remy's platinum cufflinks. "Want."

Most of the wolves had an issue with silver. For some, contact led to hives and a lot of itching. For some, it caused a full-on allergic reaction including closed-up airways and heart palpitations. Platinum wasn't an issue, though.

Remy growled.

The troll *tisked.*

He sighed and removed his links. She held out her hand but he shook his head and closed his fingers over the jewelry. "Information first."

The troll frowned. "The place you seek. It's near."

Remy withdrew his hand and dropped his links into his pocket. "You know more. I smell it on you." Remy angled his shoulders as if he was about to walk away.

"Hey!" she screeched—and swung at Remy.

In one blink of the eye, she was the small, craggy old lady holding a cup of coins, and in the next, she was as big as me.

Bigger than me. She pulled back her arm to swipe at Remy again and her knuckles raked across the chandeliers.

The tinkling of cut crystal added the casino equivalent of white noise to the room and for a split-second, it filled all the corners and crevices. The shadows winked. Remy rolled out from under her grasp. She howled and swiped with her now-huge hand to snag him around his waist.

She backhanded me with her other fist—and glued my shoulder to her hand with some sort of extruded tar. I stumbled into a bank of slots, but dug in my heels and braced against her push.

Her attention shifted from Remy to me. Her eyes narrowed, but at least she didn't howl again. She simply released whatever had stuck me to her.

It clung to my skin and my shirt. Decay halfway between compost and sulfurous rock wafted off whatever it was.

She opened her hand as if calling it back to herself.

The pull knocked me off balance. The entire bolted-together structure of slots rocked. Alarms blared. Someone near the bar yelled.

I looked up. The bartender had vanished and left her cloth and glass on the bar. The drunk sitting on the stool ignored everything. And a security guard off to the left bounced on the balls of his feet as if utterly confused.

Remy threw the troll's cup of casino coins at her face.

She danced to the side but yowled at her falling gold. A wave of the sticky stuff sprayed over Remy.

He swore. A guard yelled. The troll looked over her shoulder and pulled her tar back.

In yet another blink of the eye she returned to her little old lady glamour.

She stuck out her tongue and sprinted toward the exit.

I had no idea trolls could move so quickly. She made the glass doors before Remy made it halfway across the floor.

She looked over her shoulder, then at the dawn outside, then at us again, and I swear her face changed. What had been anger and dumb indignation switched over to the realization that she hadn't thought through her escape. That, perhaps, she'd made the wrong move.

But it was too late. She stepped onto the wide rubber mat meant to capture sand and raised her arms as if to shield her face. She was about to run outside even though she obviously knew doing so was a bad idea.

"Hey!" Remy yelled. "Don't go out into—"

The outer door hissed open. The troll stepped through.

Behind us, someone else yelled. Remy scowled but did not turn around. He ran toward the now-open door.

I turned around and held up my hands. "Grandma's been gambling too much," I said, then followed Remy and the troll out the door.

She was gone. Remy threw his hands into the air. "Stupid troll!" he yelled.

I looked back at the casino entrance. The two floor security guards stood just inside. Both watched us. "Come on," I said, and oriented Remy toward our vehicle.

He paced the sidewalk in front of the casino bent forward with his hands on his hips like a cop examining evidence. "She's gone," he finally said.

I nodded toward the guards. "We should be gone, too."

He sniffed the air. A smile replaced his anger and he made a show of slapping my shoulder. "I guess grandma's gone back to the hotel," he said.

I shrugged and walked toward where we'd parked. "So much for stealth."

Remy rubbed the back of his head and sniffed at the sleeve of his shirt. "We need showers. We can't be walking around with this stuff on our clothes."

We still carried tar residue. "It smells terrible." I pulled my shirt sleeve off my bicep. "Organic with a sulfur aftertaste." Whatever she hit us with also carried strong natural magic, which was probably why she could manipulate it with ease. But the substance was not, itself, built of magic.

"It's not low-demons," I said.

Remy flicked at a speck clinging to his shirt. "It's troll scat," he said, as if trolls threw scat every day.

I stopped mid-flick. "What?"

He pulled the keys from his pocket. "They're like monkeys." He sniffed at his shirt and made a disgusted face. "They throw their scat when they're mad."

"She flung *troll poop* at us?" I was pretty sure I now hated trolls more than Las Vegas.

Remy got in as I walked around the SUV. "It has mild psychedelic properties," he said.

I opened the passenger door. "What?" I said again. I knew nothing about trolls. We didn't have any around Alfheim, and honestly, she was the first one I'd ever met. Even my one trip to Iceland had been troll-free.

"Mild, Frank." He started the SUV. "Don't worry."

I fastened my seatbelt.

"To be honest, I didn't think she'd do something like that." Remy pulled out onto the street. "But then again, I didn't think she would run out into the morning light, either." Remy sat silent for a moment. "At least we know the apartments are nearby."

The troll had given us some useful information.

I resisted the urge to wipe the troll scat onto the SUV's seat. "Did the troll survive?" Would a troll commit suicide before talking to us?

Remy turned onto the road leading to our hotel. "Probably," he said. "She sure found you interesting with all that fake jotunn nonsense."

I chuckled. "I've been telling Arne for two centuries that I'm not a giant."

Remy laughed. "I guess we stick with paladin, then, huh?"

Paladin. "Not a paladin. Don't have Sal."

Remy laughed again. "Let's get those showers."

CHAPTER 9

Remy shouldered his bag. I shouldered mine. We looked at the minefield standing between us and the elevator to our hotel rooms.

Green and gold carpet covered with massive, semi-Egyptian themed florals rolled out before us like a gaudy yellow brick road. Above, fluorescent lights hidden in beams bounced harshness off the high, white ceilings. The occasional window and plenty of eight-foot-tall potted palms fanned out against the wide hallway's walls.

The space buzzed with chatter and a literal high-pitched whine that was part lighting, part ambient noise from the casino on the other side of the lobby behind us, and part electrical haze from the battery-operated costumes.

ElfCon festivities had already started. Turned out smaller stalls and information booths would set up the entire week, with the big events starting Thursday evening.

Tables backed by banners advertising everything from comic books to foam armor creations lined both sides of the wide walkway. Lights flashed here and there, and beeping battery-powered space weapons whooped and whistled. The distinct tang of grease paint and fried foods mingled with the over-conditioned hotel air and the troll-scat stink still on my shirt.

Remy grinned. "Looks like fun," he said.

I didn't like crowds. My patchwork body's senses didn't always pick out details well against a busy background of humans—and this background was confounded by painted faces and bright costumes. The buzzing, beeping, and laughing made it worse, as did my fatigue.

Plus I smelled of psychedelic troll scat.

"Is there another bank of elevators?" I asked. There had to be. I picked at my shirt to accent my question.

Remy shook his head. "Two hundred feet. That's it. Then we wash off the troll and take naps." He waved a hand at the people in their costumes. "This is nothing. Wait until the real elves show up."

The Conclave would start with a Feast banquet Thursday evening, as would the elven yelling. They were not a calm lot, the elves, at least not in large, political groups. But at least I knew what I was looking at when elves were in the room.

Natural magic rose off the crowd in aurora borealis updrafts. Or perhaps I was looking at the interaction of costumes and scat. "Just how psychedelic is this stuff?"

Remy closed one eye and peered at the crowd. "So many pretty colors," he said.

"Not helping, Remy." Was he seeing the updrafts, too? I squinted at a blue-painted woman in a white jumpsuit who trailed little flashes of orange and lemon yellow.

Remy chuckled and walked toward all the chatter. "You'll be fine."

The humans with painted faces were more difficult to tell apart than they should have been. "Okay, okay," I muttered, and followed him into the wide walkway full of faux creatures and critters.

Remy adjusted the strap of his bag and forged ahead. "Head down, eyes straight ahead. Walk with purpose. They will part like the Red Sea for you, my friend."

A man and a woman dressed as "elves" stared at my scars as I walked by. They both wore long blond wigs, white robes, and v-notched ringlets around their heads. Both had low pointed ears that stuck out from the sides of their heads. The man carried a tall, carved stick with a glass globe embedded in its end.

"That's all sorts of wrong," Remy said as we passed by.

No elves anywhere looked so dour and emaciated, nor were any blond. These two looked more like fashion models than fighters.

Purples drifted off the stick. Reds wafted off their fake ears. Greens off their shoulders. The white-faced superhero standing next to them cackled like a parrot. When he slapped his leg, I could have sworn I saw the wave distortion of the sound.

I stopped walking. "I think that troll hit me harder than you," I said.

One of the tables had a photo booth. A strobe flash popped and for a micro-second, the entire floor looked as if it was on fire.

Remy looked up at my face. "Okay, okay." He looked around. "I'd tell you to enjoy it, but I don't think that's possible here."

"I need to sleep this off," I said. I was no good to Remy and the search if I was seeing things I shouldn't be seeing.

Remy turned back toward the crowd, to take point. Perhaps if I stared at the back of his head, I'd get through the next two hundred feet without incident.

I looked up and over the crowd anyway, to chart our path.

To our right, between the tables, several doors to conference rooms stood open. Con-goers moved in and out, some carrying bags. Some not.

The twin Siberian elves leaned against the wall of a banquet room three doors up.

"Tell me you see them," I said. They must have flown out yesterday afternoon, to have beaten us here.

Remy glanced around. "Who?"

"The twins who locked us out of The Great Hall. They're a couple doors up on the right."

Remy stepped to the side to get a look. "Sons of bitches," he muttered. "They're probably establishing Feast enchantments ahead of the Courts' arrivals." He looked up at me. "Or they could be here because we're here."

Arne said we might not be the only ones here early. "The troll scat is making us paranoid," I said. It had to be. They were guards doing their jobs and that was it.

Remy growled a real, wolf growl. It rolled from his throat low and deep. A little kid dressed as a spaceship captain yelped and stepped toward his mother.

Remy wasn't looking at the kid. He wasn't looking at the elves, either. He was watching two tourists who were standing in front of a comic book display.

I looked at the two elves. They stopped leaning, stood up tall, and pointed.

"Remy, the twins spotted me." I towered over all the mundanes. I was surprised we'd spotted them first and not the other way around.

Remy didn't respond. He stared at the two tourists.

One of the twins walked into the banquet room. The other continued to stare directly at me. "Remy," I said.

"Tell me what you see."

He sounded much more wolf-like than I liked—much too wolf-like to be in a crowd of mundanes.

His wolf magic manifested. Remy Geroux, Alpha of the Alfheim Pack, who had moments before claimed the troll scat let him see "pretty colors," was suddenly, utterly encased in a bubble of brilliant blues, silvers, icy purples, and all things moonglow.

The colors swirled and shifted, and Remy's wolf-magic condensed into a wolf. Not a real wolf, but a bubble-ghost shimmering magic mirage of a wolf with perked-up ears, a massive ruff, and a big, fluffy tail.

"Whoa," I said. I've been out with the pack when they changed. I was aware of their moonglow wolf-magic and its ethereal shimmer that sets it apart from elven magic. But never had I seen it shape itself into a wolf.

He growled again.

"Hey," I said. "Calm down. Remember, eyes forward and head down."

He shook and blinked, and the wolf looked up at me. Not Remy. His *wolf*.

"You can't be terrorizing the mundanes," I said to the wolf. "I'm scary enough without adding you and your magic."

The wolf closed one eye and pursed his wolf lips. Then he nodded and vanished back into Remy.

"I just talked to your wolf," I said.

Remy pointed at the two tourists.

Magic swirled around them, but not like the normal shifting sheets of energy I usually saw. Their magic, like Remy's magic, wore pointy ears, snouts, and huge, fluffy tails—three tails each.

They were shorter than most of the people around them, both probably standing five and a half feet. Both looked to be Japanese, the male with short, messy hair, and the female with a long, glossy pony-tail. Both wore cargo shorts, white tube socks, and sneakers. The male had a camera on a strap around his neck, and the female carried a large camera backpack. The camera bounced against the male's garish blue, red, and green tropical-print shirt. The female's equally garish lemon-yellow polo shirt somehow shimmered more like moonlight on the ocean than the sun, but was still blindingly bright.

The male pulled a potato chip out of his fanny pack and stuck it in his mouth. The female sucked on a lollipop.

They were definitely shapeshifters.

Shapeshifters eating potato chips and sucking on a lollipop while wearing stereotypical Japanese tourist garb.

"What the hell am I looking at?" They were not at all like any spirits I'd ever seen before.

"You see the tails?" Remy asked. "Three big tails each with the white and black tips?"

"Fox tails," I said.

Remy growled again. "How did the kami know about the Conclave? No one said anything about *kitsune*."

Kitsune. Shapeshifting fox tricksters. They often worked as messengers, so even if Remy was surprised to see them here, I wasn't.

They were likely here to recon ElfCon right alongside us and the twins.

"Ignore them," I said. They probably didn't want to interact with Remy any more than he wanted to interact with them.

"Ignore them? They're kitsune. You do know that kitsune hate canines, right? We can sniff them out and we won't fall for their tricks."

"So don't fall for this one."

I glanced back at the Siberians. They were more important than two kitsune, anyway.

An elf I didn't recognize walked out of the conference room, and the twin by the door stood at attention. The twin who had gone in followed the new elf out, then stopped next to his brother, bowed his head, and pointed at me.

"We don't have time to mess with kitsune," I said. Or to figure out what they were up to.

The new elf's glamour looked minimal, at best. His ears were clearly visible, as were his deep, rich, berry-stained leathers. His trousers looked as if they'd been dipped in red wine. His thick, black, laced-up boots appeared to be military even though they were made from the same soft leather as the rest of his clothes. His jacket was a slightly lighter red than his trousers, and tied at the waist like a robe.

He was far enough away I couldn't make out his features, though his elven magic swirled around him in great curlicues of magentas, dark greens, and rich golds. And he was almost as tall as the twins.

Remy looked away from the two kitsune and at the elves. His eyes widened. "That's Niklas der Nord."

The elf grinned and waved us over.

"Who?" The only elves I knew lived in Alfheim, and though I'd met a handful of others here and there, I wasn't up on non-Alfheim politics.

"He's Siberia's Magnus—their Second in Command." Remy shifted his bag on his shoulder. "He's also Dag's ex-husband."

CHAPTER 10

Most long-lived elves marry multiple times. They have multiple families across multiple generations, often outliving children and grandchildren.

Once, in a moment of intimacy, Benta had referred to a past relationship—a husband gone three centuries, and a child—as her "ancestors." Then she closed up and never again spoke of anyone not part of her current life in Alfheim.

All the elves were like that. Magnus rarely spoke of his time as a silent movie star, and that had been only a century ago. When he did, the sense of "ancestor" permeated all his stories.

So I wasn't surprised that I knew nothing of Dag's ex-husband, though I'd always assumed that each new life was a reaction to the death of a partner. That for the elves, at least the ones I knew, remarrying was more about *moving on* than *leaving behind*.

I guess I was wrong.

"You cannot be serious, Remy," I said. The elf smiling like a shark and waving us over was Dag's ex-husband?

"I am dead serious. I only know because Gerard and I had a run-in with him when we pulled Sergei Popov into the pack."

I knew some of the Sergei story—in the sixties, while I was away at college, Sergei Popov had been part of a Soviet film crew working in the Arctic. A plane crashed. A feral wolf tore through the survivors, and by the time Gerard and Remy got to them, only Sergei had been salvageable. The Siberian elves helped to down the wolf responsible. Sergei lived with the Alfheim pack for a few years before he, too, became too feral.

Sergei Popov was now a boogeyman among the pack, a ghost wolf, and yet another reminder that the Alfheim Pack had its own little Cold War going on with Russia.

And now Niklas der Nord wanted a word.

The two kitsune turned toward us in unison. Both of their faces rounded into masks of surprise. The female in the bright yellow polo pulled her lollipop out of her mouth.

The candy at the end of the stick was shaped like a cartoon wolf. All this time, the Japanese fox spirit had been sucking on a wolf-shaped, chocolate-colored lollipop.

The male—who no longer appeared male—let out a high-pitched chittering that sounded more like a parrot imitating a car alarm than any sound a mammal should make.

They vanished. Just disappeared right in the middle of a crowd of painted and foam-board-armored mundanes as if they hadn't been there in the first place.

No one noticed. No one. Not even the three Siberians who, in my psychedelic haze, were becoming more and more shark-like.

"Remy, the kitsune are gone," I said more matter-of-factly than I was feeling.

He sniffed, then snarled. "Hate foxes," he muttered.

I grabbed him by the collar. It was one thing for me to get muddled and out of sorts while lumbering through a crowd of mundanes, but it was a whole new level of bad when a werewolf did it. "Eyes ahead. Walk fast. The elevators are right there." I pointed into the shadows. "You said this wouldn't be bad, so let's make sure it stays *not bad*, okay?"

He shook as if resetting. "Right, right," he said, but his lip continued to curl. When another group of blond fake-elven Con-goers walked by, he snarled. Thankfully, none of them noticed.

I pushed him forward. We still needed to get past the Siberians—and through the swimming colors.

Faux magic flared, swirled, and danced in hypnotic, gyrating sheets of energy around every single mundane parading between the many tables filling the annex. Every mundane in green body paint carried a red shimmer. Every pale elf sparkled with little fairy lights. Every space captain carried a swooping space travel effect.

Remy rubbed his eyes. "The kitsune," he said. "They're doing this. They made the troll scat more abundant because they do that. Make things abundant." He shook his head. "Little bastards."

"We don't know that," I said. The two kitsune might have nothing to do with the extra swirling colors. "Walk."

He stopped. "Do *not* say anything about the kitsune to the other elves. Nothing."

"Why?"

"We do not want to be associated with tricksters before a Conclave."

I glanced at the twins. "Okay," I said. I'd follow his lead on this. Seemed the wisest thing to do at the moment. Plus, it would simplify what was going to be an unwanted interaction.

We pushed through the rainbow-draped crowd as I planned what to say to Dag's ex-husband. We smelled bad, though the mundanes didn't seem to notice that, either.

The twins, now in formal black suits, white shirts, and slicked back glamour-hair, but still with their earpieces and sunglasses, stepped in front of us.

They'd switched from *Taken* to *The Matrix*. "Excellent choice of glamours, considering." I motioned to the crowd.

Mr. Left crinkled his nose.

"Please tell your boss that we ran into a troll and would like to shower before engaging in any social interactions," I said.

Mr. Right snickered. "Beer helps," he said. "Don't drink it. Use it to wash."

Mr. Left nodded. "Icelandic beer. Not that German crap."

Were they truly offering troll scat removal advice? This was possibly the most absurd situation I had ever been in during the entire two-hundred-plus years of my life.

"Thanks," I said.

"Icelanders make beer?" Remy asked. He blinked rapidly, too.

The Siberians frowned, but continued to stand stiffly in the middle of the busy walkway.

Niklas der Nord walked toward his guards. He held his shoulders straight and his hands clasped behind his back very much like the many mundane faux-supervillains walking around.

My first impression had been wrong—Niklas der Nord walked through the crowd in just enough of a glamour to make the mundanes think he wore makeup, like them. His tall ears were clearly visible, as was the silver ink of his scalp tattoos. He was Magnus-level handsome, too, with a straight nose and a strong jaw. He'd trimmed his sideburns so they matched the grooming of his well-kempt beard and waxed and curled mustache. He also wore his black hair trimmed into one of the currently popular thick-on-top styles, and it responded in the same semi-living, lifted way as every other elf's ponytail.

He extended his hand. "You are Frank Victorsson?" he asked. "Niklas der Nord, Siberian delegation and Head of Security for the Conclave. It's a pleasure."

I held up my hands to signal shaking was a bad idea. "Troll scat," I said. "I don't want to accidently transmit any."

He dropped his hand. "Wise," he said.

"We'd like to shower," I said.

He didn't move. "My emissary did not inform me of early Alfheim arrivals." He looked over his shoulder at Mr. Left, who nodded. "Everyone is to enter the Feast hall at the same time. To keep a level playing field." He pointed at the banquet room.

"We're security," Remy said. "Like you."

"King Odinsson wishes diligence," I said. "We can scent out magic elves might miss, something which can only enhance the overall security of the Courts, correct?"

Der Nord's eyes narrowed. He did not believe us. "I was under the impression that Odinsson's non-elves would be witnesses." *Witnesses* held a hint of sneer.

"Yes," I said.

"You are both witnesses *and* security?" He looked as if he was about to roll his eyes, but caught himself and decided play along, instead. "Smart," he said. "But I would expect nothing less from my Dagrun."

His Dagrun? *He's going to be a problem*, I thought.

Remy stood like a man having the same exact thoughts as me. But unlike me, Remy had a hooligan streak. "Why don't you have a ponytail like all the other elves?" he asked.

He'd paled and his eyes were dilated. The kitsune must have done something to extend the effects of the troll scat, like Remy suspected. Either they interfered, or all the ElfCon sensory stimuli were having the same effect on Remy as they were having on me.

Der Nord waved his graceful hand as if swatting away Remy's question. "Bears." He answered in much the same way as Benta had blown off Jax when he asked to see the cougars—in that offhand, blowhard way mean adults respond to children.

Remy was not impressed. "Bears?" he chortle-yipped. "*Bears*." He chortled again. "You must have barely survived."

Der Nord's lip twitched.

"Troll scat." I pointed at a speck on Remy's shirt. "I need to get him cleaned up."

Der Nord pulled a card out of his pocket. "My cell number," he said. "In case you wish to coordinate our security analyses."

I took the card.

He stepped aside. The twins looked at each other and parted like the Red Sea Remy had mentioned when we stepped into this looking glass.

I hauled Remy into the crowd. "Eyes forward," I muttered more for myself than for him. "Walk fast."

The crowd thinned near the elevators, but more people here stared at my scars and Yggdrasil tattoo than out on the floor.

I tucked der Nord's card into my pocket without looking at it and pulled out my cellphone. Arne needed to know that the Siberians were already here, and that they were aware of Remy and me.

Remy paced and blinked.

"Hit the button," I said, as I unlocked my phone's screen.

The kitsune in the tropical print shirt appeared. He—she, now—manifested from nothing right next to my left elbow.

She popped a chip into her mouth and looked down at my phone as if I was holding the world's most important fox relic.

The one in yellow appeared off to my right. She sucked on her lollipop and also stared at my phone.

Remy stopped pacing and sniffed at the air as if he smelled the kitsune, but couldn't see them.

"What is with you two?" I asked. They were clearly foxes under their shapeshifting magic. And they were sneaky.

Lollipop pointed at my phone.

I looked down at a picture I didn't take. Or didn't remember taking. A picture of a beautiful woman with a sad smile. She hugged my dog.

I had no idea who she was, though I knew I should. I had no memory of her, yet I had vague, nebulous memories of not remembering someone I should remember.

The kitsune with the chips smiled. The other one pulled her lollipop out of her mouth.

It was no longer a wolf. It was now a heart.

A shimmering, beautiful, sweet-red heart. A wonderful, psychedelically troll-scat-enhanced visual metaphor of an emotion I knew all too well.

I looked down at the photo. I couldn't remember the woman's name. I couldn't remember anything about her other than that I was all-too-aware of my inability to remember.

Remy barked. He literally *woofed* like Marcus Aurelius.

The two kitsune hissed. This time, Lollipop chittered. And they vanished once again.

They knew something. The two kitsune had information about the woman in the photo on my phone. They had to. Why else would they take such an interest?

I needed to know. I *had* to know. This not remembering—the blanks in my thoughts—they were too much like the blanks I'd suffered when I first awoke. They were holes in the world, pits into which I could all too easily trip.

Those pits frightened me.

Rage, now colored by the troll scat, took on a physicality that was eerily similar to the oily, sticky residue of low-demons.

How many times had I forgotten the woman in the picture already? How many times had the fear surfaced and I not realized? Because when my fear surfaced, so did my rage.

"You leave the foxes alone!" I bellowed at Remy.

Two new, blond fake-elves gasped as they walked by.

"And you two!" I poked the air in their general direction. "You look ridiculous!"

They backed away.

I pointed at Remy. "Elevator!" I snapped.

He bared his teeth.

The Siberians were pushing their way toward us through the crowd in the wide hallway.

I looked back at the elevator.

A woman stood between me and the button. She was the same height as Remy, with long, sleek, black hair which she'd tied off into two low braids with equally black rawhide. She watched me with impassive, deep brown, almost black eyes from a sharply featured, lovely face.

I recognized her. She'd been behind the bar at the casino. At the time, I hadn't seen her magic.

Like the kitsune fox magic—like Remy's wolf magic—her magic carried a specific shape, one that without the troll scat, I knew I would have difficulty picking out against the backdrop of her functional magic.

Or maybe it was my faulty-memory-caused rising blood pressure. Either way, her wings were fully, gloriously visible.

She must have known at the casino that I hadn't figured out who or what she was. She clearly knew I understood now.

What did Maura say before I left Alfheim? Beware the tricksters.

The spirit who was Raven grinned, then she, too, vanished.

I blinked. The walls wavered.

I roared.

And I punched my fist all the way through wallboard into the empty spaces underneath.

CHAPTER 11

I punched a hole in the wall. I'd almost put a hole in my new truck, too.

Too many stimuli. Too much happening. Too many magicals looking to mess with my head. I tucked my phone into my pocket and inhaled deeply.

Rage, I thought. This wasn't low-demons. This was me being *me*. Buzzed-out and overwhelmed, but still me.

Water shot out of a cracked pipe behind the hole. The jet arced over the elevator waiting area and directly into a potted palm on the opposite wall. Thank Odin's plucked-out eyeball I hadn't hit electrical, too.

Remy stared at the stream as if it was a rainbow and he was its leprechaun.

There had to be stairs nearby. Maybe pulling Remy up fifteen flights of stairs would be enough to burn off the magic-enhanced troll-visions. I ducked under the stream of water and checked around a half-wall on the other side of the elevators.

Sigils appeared between the water jet and the crowd.

The water stopped flowing. It shimmered like a river just before ice forms—like autumn's first kiss of winter—and froze solid.

Mr. Left and Mr. Right walked into the elevator waiting area and took up positions on either side of Remy and me. Niklas der Nord followed.

Gently and with great reverence, he touched the arch of frozen water.

It shattered. Crystals rained down onto the carpet in a twinkling symphony of harmonics.

He placed his hands behind his back again like a self-righteous supervillain. "Are you always this much of a threat to the world around you, Mr. Victorsson?"

My arm wanted to swing. My shoulder wanted to punch. My throat wanted to bellow and my fingers wanted to snap his elf neck.

Der Nord shook his head. "Arne Odinsson thinks he keeps you under control, doesn't he?" He took a step toward Remy. "Just like those vampires."

Remy shook again, and he oriented his entire body to der Nord. "Careful with your insults," he said.

"Insults? I'm not the one who stumbled around Las Vegas and got myself troll-scatted because I shamble haphazardly into dangerous situations."

Niklas der Nord was looking for a fight. I wouldn't give it to him, but that didn't mean I would concede defeat.

"Are you two his shining examples of Alfheim?" he *tsked*.

Mr. Left stiffened. Mr. Right's expression showed clear surprise.

They weren't der Nord's full-time guards. They wouldn't be surprised by his behavior if they were—or his arrogance had finally crested over their tolerance.

Remy walked right into der Nord's personal space. "Was it polar bears that got your magic mane? Too much glare off the glaciers, huh? The bare nakedness of the Arctic too shiny for your sweet elf eyes? Puts you in hairy situations. How do you bear the burden? Those polar bears must have been barely visible." Remy peered at der Nord's ears. "A polar bear would have ripped those pristine ears and that hipster 'stache right off your pretty elf head."

"Remy…" I reached for him, but he dodged.

"Or did you mean 'bear' metaphorically?" Remy tapped his chin. "Did you lose big in the markets and have to sell your hair?" He nodded toward the twins. "Which is it, boys?"

Neither guard responded.

Remy dropped into a bad Australian accent. "Koalas come at'cha, mate?"

The twins alternated between angry stares and holding in snickers.

Der Nord crossed his arms. "Koalas aren't bears," he said.

Remy swirled his finger in front of der Nord's nose. "And *you* aren't a *king*."

Der Nord pushed Remy away. Remy drunkenly sidestepped and came back around to der Nord's shoulder. "Such pristine ears. No stories here," he said, then stepped back. "I bet the twins have ears that tell tales."

He stepped right up to der Nord again. "You don't have enough scars to be King."

Niklas der Nord raised his hands to hit Remy with a full blast of magic, but Remy danced out of the way.

Remy leaned forward. He tightened his back and hunched his shoulders.

His wolf magic once again formed around his human shape.

I pointed at Mr. Left. "Your boss made the choice to escalate this situation even though he was fully aware that we had been attacked by a troll."

The guard held perfectly still. No twitches. No acknowledgements. He neither moved to help nor hinder.

I pulled Remy toward the stairs. "Come on."

He snarled at the elves. "*Woof*," he said.

I yanked him around the low wall and into the stairwell. The door hissed closed behind us.

The halogen light in the stairwell bounced equally off all the surfaces—the shiny red-painted metal railings, the tight green weave of the carpet, and the dull textured beige wallpaper. I squinted and pushed Remy toward the steps.

He rolled his shoulders and grinned menacingly. "Who's afraid of the big bad wolf?" he said.

"Don't get cocky." The last thing we needed was to ignite an elf-wolf war. "We have a job to do, remember? We're here to protect Arne, not make matters worse."

Remy bounded up the steps. "You know, I honestly thought Portia Elizabeth would show up the moment we landed."

He took the corner and ran up the next flight.

"Why?" If she hadn't contacted him in three centuries, why would she start now?

He stopped and looked over the railing. "I was her favorite."

I rounded the corner and started up the next flight. "Can you hear yourself?" I asked.

Maybe the elves had a point with all the "ancestor" business. An elf would never get so caught up in the past.

Remy looked up into the spiral above our heads. "You're the one who broke a pipe."

He wanted to change the subject. Obviously, thoughts of Portia Elizabeth raised too many uncomfortable memories...

Memories. I pulled out my phone.

"Remy." I stopped two steps down and held out my phone. "Do you know this woman?"

He peered at the photo. "No. Should I?"

I had no idea. I carried no memory of him or any of the wolves meeting her any more than I carried memories of *me* meeting her.

Frustration pushed up from my gut again. "Those two kitsune insinuated that she's important to me." They insinuated a lot more than simple importance.

Remy pointed at my nose. "They mess with lonely men. You stay away from them."

"I am not lonely," I snapped.

"*Sure.*" Remy started up the steps again.

"You're the one who thought your three-hundred-year-old affair with a succubus would restart the moment you set foot in Las Vegas."

He turned around again. "You fell right back into bed with Benta the Nameless."

"That was her idea." It was. I should have listened to my gut and sent her home.

Remy laughed. *"Right."*

Benta wasn't happening again, anyway. I held out my phone again. "I need to know who *this* woman is."

Remy walked backward up the steps. *"We* need to find Portia Elizabeth. You heard Niklas der Nord down there. Do you really want him deposing Arne? Because that's what he wants. You know I'm right."

Referring to Dag as his, the fact that he was Siberia's elder elf, his insinuation that Alfheim needed control, the calling of a Conclave...

Remy was correct. We had a usurper on our hands.

"That bastard will rip Alfheim apart if he gets his way." He turned around. "He'll destroy my pack. He'll take Akeyla away from Jax. He'll send away Axlam."

And he'd toss me out, too.

"You will never figure out who she is if you lose access to the elves," Remy said.

He was right. Finding Portia Elizabeth needed to be our priority.

I followed him up the stairs to our rooms.

CHAPTER 12

Room service carried beers from every nation on the planet except Iceland, so I didn't bother with an order and cleaned off the troll scat with the hotel-provided "fresh scented" moisturizing body bar instead. I suspected it didn't do a one-hundred-percent thorough job, but at least I was free of the obvious traces.

I stuffed my scat-tainted clothes into one of the hotel-provided plastic bags, rolled it over, stuffed the bundle into a trash liner, rolled that, then used another liner to tie it shut. I'd hand over the bundle to elves when I got home and let them do the necessary decontamination.

I shaved not only my chin but also the sides of my scalp, figuring that clearly presenting my elf-created Yggdrasil tattoo while der Nord and the twins were around might help them to understand my integration into Alfheim. I also lined up a few stories about how the tracers and protection enchantments—both of which had been stolen by my brother—had served me well while I carried them, including how they helped Dag find us in the Carlson house fire and had allowed me to carry out Akeyla.

Would my stories help garner at least some respect? I doubted it. But I would try.

Remy met me in the hall. Our rooms were directly across from one another, separated by a moat of golden-green industrial carpet and a bright circle of halogen glare. He tucked his t-shirt into his jeans as he pulled the door closed.

Remy, like me, preferred dark cotton t-shirts, most unembellished, and sturdy denim. He'd picked a navy blue shirt where I'd picked a dark burgundy, so at least we wouldn't be walking the hotel unintentional twins.

He held out his phone. "Looks like we have thirteen advertised apartment complexes near the casino where we met our scat-throwing friend."

I glanced at the map and nodded.

Remy tucked the phone into his pocket as we walked toward the elevator. "My initial guess was that the building in question would *not* advertise for mundane renters, but then I thought what better cover? Half the units to mundanes, and half to magicals."

"Or we're looking for a smaller building with no mundanes," I said.

He shrugged. "Either way, we have a place to start."

The first building, about two blocks north of the troll's casino, turned out to be a dump that looked more like a rundown hotel than an apartment building. Paint peeled off the concrete pillars. The metal supports on the balconies rusted to the point we could see the damage from the road. No magic lifted off the structure. No incidental ribbons. No shadows indicating a magical lived there.

The second building was a gated high-rise behind palm trees and was too far from the street for me to get a good visual reading. Remy made a note and we moved on.

The next two buildings faced each other across a pool. People milled about, and cars filled the lot off to one side, but I didn't get any sense of any magicals.

Same with our fourth, fifth, and sixth complexes.

We pulled up outside stop seven. The desert heat pooled in the early evening sun, inside the soon-to-pop bubble of the day's retained sunshine. Glare off the pavement was at its worst, with the lowering angle of the sun. The world was about to transition to night, and it made the air tap its foot and fidget its fingers.

Remy's stomach rumbled. I'd been fighting hunger pangs for about an hour. This would be our last stop for the day, then back to the hotel for dinner, some spying on the elven security detail, and a prowl through the casinos in hopes of catching a local magical working a table or two.

I peered at the prefab tan stucco entrance. A parking lot spanned one entire side of the building, and a fenced pool filled the other.

"Nothing," I said.

Remy sighed.

"Perhaps the concealment enchantments are stronger than we thought."

He rubbed at his hair. "*Hmmm...*"

He wasn't looking at me. He stared at the tall concrete wall across the road.

I didn't see any magic lifting off whatever stood behind the fence. "What?"

"Foxes," he muttered.

All I saw was concrete. "Here?"

Remy hopped out of our rental SUV, looked both ways, and walked toward the wall.

From across the street, its sand-colored paint made it fade into the background even though the wall was a fifteen-foot-tall cinderblock monstrosity that looked more like the outer fence of a prison than any housing development noise barrier.

I followed Remy to the other side of the street.

Up close, the rustling of the tops of palm trees on the other side muted the prison effect. Laughter drifted up as well, as did splashing, and the scent of chlorinated water.

"There's a pool on the other side," I said.

His nose twitched and he looked up and down the block.

No gates were visible.

Remy nodded toward the west. "You go that way."

"We are not splitting up. Not if you smell kitsune." Those two brats were probably hoping for some divide-and-conquer action.

"Fine," Remy said. "We could jump the wall." He pointed at the top of the concrete fence.

"And deal with the Las Vegas police?" Nothing caused 911 calls faster than a werewolf scaling a wall in full daylight.

We walked east, hoping to find an entrance. Remy trotted along the sidewalk, with me following.

The visible treetops spread out, then vanished completely as we moved along the wall. The tiled roof of a building became visible once we rounded the first corner, but no gates, and no driveway, though we both heard cars inside.

Around the third corner, the fence jogged inward around a telephone pole and an array of electrical junctions, but still no gate.

When our SUV came back into sight, Remy stopped. He slapped the wall and pointed at the flat, unadorned top of the wall. "Seems we found what we were looking for."

This had to be the apartment complex Mark Ellis mentioned, but we couldn't get in. We couldn't introduce ourselves and we couldn't ask questions.

Clearly, we were not welcome.

Remy slapped the wall again. He shook his head. "Sorry to offend!" he called. "Let's get dinner." He pointed at the SUV.

I glanced at our ride. When I glanced back, the wall was gone.

Not the full wall. We were standing in the dead center of a wide driveway flanked on either side by open, tall, mesh-filled, utilitarian steel gates. When closed, they'd stop not just a car, but also foot traffic.

A yellow and black electronic pass scanner stood so close to my elbow I was surprised I hadn't bumped into it.

And in the middle of the driveway, between the open gates, sat a dark-haired woman with braids. She wore jeans and a t-shirt much like ours, and big, black, military-style boots. Black-lensed sunglasses covered her eyes, and a huge straw hat with ragged edges, her head.

She crossed her legs and tapped her beer against her blue camp chair.

"Raven," I said.

Two hundred years in North America and this was the first time a native spirit deemed me worthy of a conversation—and my gut said this conversation was not about to go well.

"I figured when that troll said 'nearby' you two would show up sooner or later." She sipped at her beer. "Then those two Japanese foxes had to get *you* all riled up." She pointed the beer at Remy.

His eyes widened. I nodded as if to say *She's exactly who you think she is.*

He quickly regained his composure and bowed. "It's an honor, Madame Raven."

She laughed. "Yes, it is." She sipped at her beer again. "They're not here, by the way. You're sniffing other spirits who would rather be left alone."

He lifted his hands as if to signal defeat. "I meant no harm."

Raven set her beer on the ground. "Now that, right there, is a lie."

Remy dropped his hands, but thankfully did not argue.

"Those two kitsune get a kick out of messing with you," she said, "and the wolf in you wants to shake them until they stop that obnoxious, chittering screech they make." She pushed her sunglasses up her nose.

This conversation would spiral into something Remy would regret if I didn't derail it right now. "We're not here about the kitsune," I said.

Raven stood. She dusted her knees and stretched her back.

Her wings erupted behind her in full, magical detail—huge, black, and feathered. They spanned the entire width of the driveway from gate to gate, shimmering in the low evening sun. Rainbows danced through their feathers. Fluttering and flapping drowned out all other noises, and I swear, somewhere in the distance, I heard cawing.

Then her wings, in all their magical glory, vanished.

"I wish to pose a question to you two gentlemen." She walked toward us. "How do you believe your target remembers her time in your glorious northern land?"

I looked at Remy. He looked at me. She knew we were looking for Portia Elizabeth.

But of course she knew. All Raven myths carried acknowledgement of a corvid's intelligence and cleverness. She probably had a better understanding of the big picture than anyone in Las Vegas, Remy and I included.

He shook his head. "I wish I knew," he said. "I wish I remembered."

He didn't know. That much was obvious from our conversation on the plane. I suspected that *not* knowing felt, to him, the same way the not knowing about the woman on my phone felt to me—like a hole in my map of the world.

Raven walked right up to Remy. She stopped inches away, and pulled off her sunglasses. "You've looked for her before, haven't you?" She tipped her head to the side. "Every time you go out to fetch a stray, you look." She sniffed at his face. "But this is your first sanctioned search. Neither your brother nor your King wanted to tempt a chaotic fate once again, so you've been sneaky."

This chasing after Arne's ace in the hole was, for Remy, more than helping his town and pack. It was a search for understanding.

Raven stepped back. "Three hundred years of *not* reaching out —*not* asking if there was anything her ex-community could do to help her—but the moment the Elf King of Alfheim needs *her* help it's all 'let's chase down the female fertility spirit.'"

"It's not that simple," Remy whispered.

"Oh yes it is, young man." Raven tapped him between the eyes. "It very much is *that simple*."

"She's dangerous," Remy said.

"And you're not?" She tapped his chest. "You have no idea the fate you tempt here, boy."

Remy's lip curled.

"We are done speaking of your target." Raven snapped his mouth with her fingers before he could get out a word. "You are done searching. Do you understand? No stalking, wolf boy."

He sniffed and pulled his head back and his lips off her fingers, but thankfully kept his mouth shut.

She walked over to me and looked up at my face. "My, aren't you a big one. Jotunn big." She tapped my chest. "You are a fascination, Mr. Victorsson. A new creature. One shiny and interesting." She winked.

There had to be something I could offer. Some sort of exchange, so that we could get the information we needed. "I am at your service, Madame Raven," I said.

I don't know why I said it. I don't know why a call to help struck me here, in the middle of a parted concealment enchantment in Las Vegas. I don't know why the sins of the past and the fears of the future made me want to reach out, but they did.

If I was going to figure this out, I needed as much help as everyone around me.

"*Never* offer services to a trickster," Remy hissed.

Raven whipped around. "Too late."

She placed her hand on my chest. "Interesting. You have walked in The Land of the Dead."

"I have," I said. My brother pulled me into The Land of the Dead when he became fixated on destroying my life.

She touched my cheek. "And you have withstood a... piercing dark magic, yes?"

Arne told me I carried no residual magic from the pike my brother —Dracula, after the vampire lord took control of Brother's body— rammed through my chest, yet the spirit of Raven sensed some sort of lasting effect. "I am clean of that magic," I said.

"You are, son of Victor." She lifted her hand off my cheek and rubbed her fingers together as if feeling the dust of my soul. "You and I will talk again."

Raven vanished. Her beer and chair vanished. The gates creaked and groaned, and closed us out of the complex.

Remy rubbed his face. He turned in a circle and looked up at the sky. Then he stomped back to the SUV.

Why did my gut tell me that I was about to regret offering my services to a trickster spirit? Part of me wondered if Portia Elizabeth did the same thing three centuries ago.

I touched the metal of the gate and yanked back my hand from the heat. The air around it swirled like a watery mirage, and pushed me away.

I stepped back just as the wall reformed. I ran my finger over the scratchy, sandy "cinderblock." We wouldn't be talking to anyone inside, at least not tonight.

Remy called from across the street.

"I'm coming," I said, and touched the wall again. The enchantment was as solid as the concrete it imitated. There was nothing I could do against magic like that.

I walked back to the SUV. "Now what?" I asked.

Remy started the vehicle. "We get food and we plan."

CHAPTER 13

R emy chewed his burger. Behind us, out on the floor, lights
popped and bells dinged. We sat in a raised restaurant area just
off the casino, in a spot with a good view of the main walkway corridor. Our table butted up against the polished brass railing separating
the players from the eaters.

A guest out in the casino, behind the slots and the games, whooped
and a crowd cheered.

"Somebody won," I said.

Remy sipped his beer and ignored the gaming joy of the
mundanes. "See any magic?"

He'd been asking the same questions every ten minutes since we
came down for dinner.

I shook my head. Nothing beyond a few people with higher-than-
average natural magic, all of whom were likely touched and not
magical in any way. Remy frowned and took another bite of his
burger.

A lovely young woman in a fluttery and expensive dress walked up
to our table. She leaned against the brass rail and smiled at Remy.
"Hello," she said. "You two look lonely."

Remy grinned back. "We're here on our honeymoon. Isn't that right, muffin?"

I smiled sweetly.

She shrugged. "Well, if you two change your minds, I'll be around." She walked away in search of another mark.

I chewed my final bite of burger. "Didn't you have a girlfriend with a cat named Muffin?"

"Mr. Cuddle-muffin Fluffy-butt." Remy wiped his fingers. "At least she didn't have a fox."

He was still fixating on the kitsune. Wolves, when they got a target in their sights, didn't give up until the target was brought down, or in the case of werewolves, until someone dragged their sorry backsides back to Alfheim.

And here in Las Vegas, Remy had multiple targets in his sights—the kitsune, Raven, and Portia Elizabeth—and he rotated between them depending on how indignant he felt at any given moment.

Such was the way of the wolves. I would not interfere. The wolves' way got the job done the vast majority of the time, so there had to be some value to indignant rotation as a hunting strategy.

Except now. Raven made it clear—as clear as a trickster spirit is going to make anything—that we were on our own from this point forward. Any asking for help from Portia Elizabeth was going to fall on deaf ears.

I scanned the casino again. "We need to concentrate on how we're going to present ourselves at the Conclave Feast," I said.

"Why?" Remy watched a high roller swagger by flashing gold chains and rings.

"Because Raven put an end to our investigation." Fixations usually didn't block the obvious for most of the wolves, but Remy seemed particularly annoyed.

Remy pushed a pickle to the side before munching on a fry. "Raven is a trickster." He sipped his soda. "And fascinated with you."

I sat back. "She's Raven. I'm shiny and interesting." I was beginning to think magicals, as a whole, had fixation issues. The elves were pretty much live and let live, though.

Remy laughed. "Watch out. She'll steal your car keys."

"Not this Raven," I said.

He watched another couple walk by. "I don't think she's a regular Raven spirit," he said.

So Remy's instincts mirrored my own. "She wants us to leave Portia Elizabeth alone." Why did he feel he needed to argue with a spirit, especially a major spirit? Arguing with a spirit wasn't all that different from arguing with an elf—you weren't going to win. "Maybe we should listen."

But Remy was an Alpha werewolf, and arguing with a fixated Alpha wolf wouldn't get me anywhere, either.

I was beginning to wonder if sending Remy had been Arne's wisest move. I'd have no idea what I was doing, though, if I'd come alone.

"Want me to call Arne?" I asked. We'd already made Alfheim aware of the Niklas der Nord situation. Not the Raven interaction, though. "Maybe Axlam can fly down. She's good with diplomacy. Perhaps Raven would take better to a female werewolf." Portia Elizabeth, if she did come forward, might do better with Remy's sister-in-law.

He stared out into the casino. "Why have Raven step in? Why not tell me herself?" he muttered.

This was not a path I wished to take—this ruminating about his worthiness to speak to the fertility spirit who once loved him. Not now. Not in a room full of swirling roulette tables and drunks playing blackjack. Not ever, to be honest. Remy's issues were his own.

An old, fat man with thinning, slicked-back hair groped a young woman as they walked by.

"Now that, right there," Remy pointed, "is messed up *and* boring." He pushed back his chair. "I'm going back to the apartments. Maybe I'll find someone who knows something. Someone who isn't a trickster."

"What are you going to do?" The gate into the complex was hidden. "Don't jump the wall, Remy." Either he'd need to pick up gear or he'd have to shift to his wolf form. "The last thing we need is for you to go fully four-legged and howling while der Nord is out there looking for any excuse to point out the great incivility of Alfheim."

"I don't think you understand the severity of the situation," Remy said.

Of course I understood. "Arne wants a powerful dark magical to walk into the Feast, wink at the elves, and declare diplomatic parity with Alfheim and her Court."

Remy sighed. "Yes, yes, Arne Odinsson, the tamer of the non-elven and bringer of great economic prosperity." He shook his head. "That's not the whole picture."

I frowned. "Without a show of strength from the Alfheim Court, we might just end up with a new, unfriendly king."

Remy tapped the table. "Do you know why Tyr Bragisson is the Elf Emperor and not the Norwegian King? Why it is that the eight Scandinavian enclaves throughout Norway, Sweden, Finland, and Denmark are under one ruler? Why the smaller enclaves in England and France don't have their own kings? Because they should."

I knew some of the story. "There was an elf who called himself Lokisson." And Loki's purpose was to spread chaos.

Remy nodded. "This was in the early sixteen hundreds, right about the time Gerard and I caught a ship to the New World." He sighed. "We were still pretty wild back then, though we held ourselves well enough to travel with mundanes and not kill the entire crew."

I'd often wondered how they managed crossing on sailing ships.

"One of the reasons we left was because Tov Lokisson had gotten control of two of the Scandinavian enclaves and was waging all-out war on the other European groups. We didn't want to get caught in the crossfire."

"How many non-elves did Lokisson take down?" I asked. A trickster elf might explain the long-held issues between the European werewolves and the elves.

Remy looked out at the casino. "Enough," he said.

Enough to drive out the brothers.

"The Siberian enclave was established in much the same way as Alfheim—a bunch of Rus decided to see how far inland they could get. In the sixteen hundreds, they were isolated from the other elves by the Romanov Dynasty. The Icelanders were also outside the war, and

Alfheim was the most isolated of all. The European elves knew it existed, but no one put in the considerable effort needed to visit."

Some things never changed. They still didn't visit.

Remy reached for a toothpick. "Tyr Bragisson recognized the threat Tov Lokisson posed not only to the elves, but to the mundanes. He coordinated with the Siberians and together, they took care of the problem."

He tapped the toothpick against the table too fast, as if nervous. "Now all of the Scandinavian enclaves are ruled by one central King. Siberia and Iceland gained significant political power, and Alfheim was brought back into the fold, a deal solidified when Tyr sent Dag to marry Arne."

Yes, the elves were political. Yes, control shifted. "I don't understand how Tyr Bragisson becoming the Elf Emperor applies to you scaling the walls of an enchantment-protected apartment complex."

Remy dropped the toothpick and picked up a fork. He twirled it between his fingers. "That video? The one your brother made of Akeyla breaking glamour? Imagine what would happen if that particular bit of modern mundane technology caught the eye of a new Lokisson."

No one needed a Loki-level trickster playing with a shiny bobble at the end of an Internet string.

"The elves no longer tolerate tricksters. Not their own and not anyone else's." Remy poked the fork into the table. "Which, I believe, is the true root of their problem with witches, vampires, and iffy spirits. The elves don't want another Lokisson issue."

"And Arne is taking in the enemy." None of this was a surprise. The other enclaves wanted to extend their no-trickster rule.

It made sense on the surface. Actually, it made a lot of sense, but it was a simplistic way of dealing with a complex matter, and simplistic diplomacy did not get you a new enclave in New Zealand.

Remy tapped the table. "Now think about what's going to happen when Niklas der Nord gets wind of Raven's involvement in our investigations." He waved the fork between us. "And how we bowed to her wishes."

This was why he didn't want me to mention the kitsune.

We'd be viewed as trickster enablers. I sat back. "He'd do that?" But of course he'd do that. He'd already vocalized his bigotry.

Remy exhaled. "That's just the beginning. He's going to use the fact that we are here at all against Arne. Then top that with a failed search for a dark magical."

Remy was right to be fixated.

"Raven was correct," he said. "I have been looking for Portia Elizabeth since she left Alfheim. I comb every location we visit. I gather information every time we get a call to pick up someone who's been turned. Gerard knows." He glanced at me. "Arne, too."

"But you didn't know to look here, did you?" He would have been on a plane the moment he had a solid lead.

Remy shook his head. "Yet somehow, Arne knew." He looked out at the casino floor again. "I asked point blank how he knew, the moment he told me he wanted us to fly in first." His brow tightened. "He was cagey. Said only that he 'called in a few favors.' He and I are going to have a talk when this is through. I want to know who, exactly, owes Arne Odinsson favors. I want to know what he's gotten Alfheim into."

"We can't worry about that now," I said. "We had a more immediate problem on our hands."

"We have two choices: Canvas here and see if we get lucky, or go back to the apartments and state our case again."

Neither option was good. "We *ask*, Remy. No breaking and entering."

He laughed and tossed a tip onto the table. "Won't need to, since you offered up yourself as a sacrifice."

I stood and stretched my back. "I did no such thing."

Remy laughed again. "You take the paladin service thing way too seriously, Frank."

It worked for me. I preferred to be the helpful giant instead of the raging, terrifying monster. "I've learned my lessons over my two centuries."

We walked toward the little food area's exit. Remy pulled our rental's keys out of his pocket. "I suppose someone needs to learn something from immortality, huh?"

He was probably correct. I just hoped we were wise enough to handle another round at the apartments with diplomacy and intelligence.

CHAPTER 14

"Ready?" Remy pulled the keys from the rental's ignition.

The sun had set about half an hour ago, and a faint red glow pulsed along the horizon. The apartment complex's fifteen-foot-high concrete fence continued to appear formidable—and continued to not have any visible entrances.

We knew where the driveway was, even if we couldn't see it. We knew it had an electronic gate card system. Such systems were always hooked up to an intercom of some sort.

"I hope you're right about there being someone on the other end of the intercom," Remy said.

"We need to find it first," I said.

Remy reached into the back seat and pulled two bundles into the front—my scat-covered clothes, and his.

"You, my friend, are a stronger man than I," Remy said.

This had nothing to do with strength and everything to do with my ability to see magic. We both figured a little extra push from the troll droppings might just be enough to allow me to see the driveway and the intercom.

I took the bundles, and the three extra plastic bags I was to use to re-seal the clothes, once I'd inhaled enough troll leavings to boost my abilities.

"Do you know how I know trolls aren't too bright?" Remy pointed at the bundles. "They could have all the gold in the world if they figured out how to refine and sell that."

I suspected somewhere on Earth, some troll had. "We should all be happy they haven't."

Remy sat back in his seat. "Tap the window when you're ready."

I opened my door and walked around the SUV to stand on the street side next to Remy's closed window, to protect him from the scat. Quickly, I ripped a hole though the plastic around my clothes, and inhaled.

The concrete wall sparkled. The streetlights burned. But no driveway.

I ripped a hole in the bags holding Remy's clothes and inhaled again.

Waves of reds, blues, and purples moved through sheets of energy in the sky above the city. The concrete wall's sparkles turned into a buzzing, spinning web of fairy lights.

It wasn't fifteen feet tall. More like five. The height was a magical illusion, as was the "wall" crossing the driveway.

I quickly re-bundled the clothes inside the new layers of plastic and tapped the glass. Remy powered down the driver's side window.

"It's right there." I pointed across the street.

The entire steel gate structure shimmered with greens, blues, and purples as if anodized by a mermaid. Behind it, the drive twisted between two huge palms and into a parking lot that bordered the wall next to the entrance. Two smallish two-story buildings, each with six apartments, sat at a right angle against the eastern and northern sides of the wall. The pool and a pool house butted up against the wall to the west.

Remy hopped out and hit the lock on the SUV. "Let's do this."

We walked across the road and up to the driveway, Remy in front and me carrying the troll scat bundle in case I needed more.

The reader clung to another anodized pole and presented a black face to anyone holding out a correctly magnetized card. Our target button waited in the top corner, as a small, yellow depression labeled "Help."

Carefully, I touched the reader's metal case—and yanked back my hand. "It's ice cold," I said. "Full depth-of-winter frozen dead cold."

Remy sniffed even though he could neither see nor smell the reader. "Where's the button?"

I pointed.

He tried to push it, but each jab missed the mark by a good foot.

The spell was distorting space. His hand moved correctly, except he was punching his finger at an optical illusion and his entire hand flew by the reader.

I handed him the scat bundle, pulled my t-shirt out of my jeans, wrapped the fabric around my hand, and poked at the yellow intercom button.

A loud, discordant bell rang. Remy cringed. I closed my eyes as if not looking at the gate's magic would help keep the jarring noise at an acceptable level.

Crackling popped from the card reader. "Who rang that bell?" a deep, slow, male voice asked.

Remy leaned closer even though he had no idea what he leaned into. "We did. We're looking for—"

"Can't you read the sign?" the bored voice said.

"What sign?" I asked. The entire gate and driveway area lacked signage of any type—no sign in big, script font declaring the complex "Vegas Springs" or "Desert Meadows" or whatever else a builder might name an apartment complex. No "keep out" or "keep off" sign on the gate, either. No marks on the driveway. Just the yellow "Help" button on the card reader.

The voice sighed. "The notice. It's as plain as the noses on your faces."

No, it wasn't. Were we dealing with another trickster?

"Do you see a sign?" Remy asked.

"We're looking for Portia Elizabeth," I said to the card reader. "Is there someone on the premises who could get a message to her for us?"

"Portia Elizabeth?" The voice continued his slow and bored drawl. "Stop wasting my time."

"Please," Remy said. "I'm one of the Alfheim Pack Alphas. We need to speak to her. It's important."

The crackling turned into a hiss. "Prove it," the voice said.

Remy pulled out his wallet. "We have Minnesota driver's licenses and Alfheim addresses." He waved his license as if it would trigger the card reader.

"Well, bust my buttons," the voice drawled. "How special for you."

"Look," I said. "All we want is to leave a message and our contact information. That's all." I walked toward the gates and looked inside. No signs beyond the gate, either. A small building between the driveway and the pool had to be the office, though.

"Your contact information, huh?" the voice said. "Nothing else?"

"Yes," Remy answered.

"Because we don't need Big Elf coming around here."

I looked over my shoulder. *Big Elf*, I mouthed?

Remy scoffed. "Big Elf?"

"Yeah," the voice said. "Big Elf. Big Kami. Big Fae. We don't need your rules, man."

Remy pinched his mouth shut as he tried to hold in a laugh. "No one wants Big Fae around, my friend. *No one.*"

"Yeah," said the voice.

We were making progress. I waved the troll scat bundle at Remy.

He nodded. "Hey," he said. "How about a trade? We have troll scat. You'd see Big Fae coming a mile away with this stuff."

The hissing continued. Sounds of rustling followed. "How much?"

"Two sets of contaminated clothes."

Another moment passed. "Is it the good stuff?"

"We found the gate, didn't we?" I said.

"Why didn't you say you had scat in the first place?" the voice said. "That's a whole different breed of mare, my friends."

The gate groaned. Wheels turned, and it creaked open. "Come on in!"

Remy squinted. "I don't see it."

He had no idea where to walk. "Close your eyes." I gripped his arm and led him toward the wild swirls of yellows, oranges, and pinks that filled the air where the concealment enchantment crossed the driveway.

"Whoa." Remy jerked and danced as if poked by cattle prods. "It's like touching a livewire."

Energy crackled over us. Remy's short hair stood on end, and the small hairs on my arms stood straight. The static wormed its way into my scars, into my muscles, and all the way to my bones. Each step bit at the soles of my feet. Each push forward felt as if it was about to fry off my skin.

Three strides. That was all. Three steps and Remy and I stood on the other side of the gate, in the middle of the paved entrance, with normal cars on one side and two normal, if somewhat rundown, apartment buildings in front of us. The buildings sat perpendicular to each other, with the cinderblock side of the east-facing unit closest. All six apartments of both buildings opened onto walkways, very much like a hotel. Balconies dotted the backs.

Kids played in the pool. Adults chatted. The complex was a normal, everyday place, except for the magic drifting out of most, but not all, of the apartment doors.

Remy pointed at the office. "We start there?"

Waves of reds, yellows, and magentas drifted out around the small building's big windows, and under its door. Its tile roof shimmered in the afternoon sun. Chlorine and humidity wafted off the pool behind the office in equally great smelled and unseen waves. On the other side of the gate, cars passed by.

Without the magic, this place would be any random apartment complex anywhere.

I nodded and started toward the office door.

Two teenagers in swimsuits rounded the corner of the building. The boy dried the top of his head with a towel as brightly swirling as the magic around him. The younger girl wrapped her own towel around her waist. Their dark hair and eyes, the oval shape to both their faces, and their almost identical, sinewy builds suggested that they were siblings.

They looked like mundanes. No overt glamour hid any signs of elf, kami, or fae, but natural magic coiled off both of them in a flickering dance of sunlight and cold shadow.

The boy put out his hand to stop his sister. "Werewolf," he said.

Remy extended his hand. "Remy Geroux, Alfheim Pack Alpha." He nodded to me. "Frank Victorsson, Alfheim's resident jotunn."

The girl frowned. "Jotunn?" she said. "You better be careful."

"I think you need to stop telling people that, Remy," I said.

The girl's magic snapped outward. One tentacle quickly touched my forehead, and another, Remy's.

She grabbed her brother's arm. "They know Mark!"

The boy wrapped his towel around his neck. "Mark Ellis?" He stepped closer, even though he was obviously still wary. "He lived here for a few months a year back."

Remy stuck his hands into his back pockets and smiled one of his most charming smiles at the kids. "He's joined our pack. He's studying to become a police officer."

The boy scoffed. "Mark? A cop?"

The girl crossed her arms. "Did you two have anything to do with that magical gate that opened up a few days ago? The one Anthea went through?"

Did one of Dracula's gates into Vampland open here? "Anthea?" I asked.

"Thea's a vampire," the girl said. "But she's nice."

I looked at Remy. He looked at me. "A good vampire?" he asked.

The boy shrugged. "I don't know about *good*, but she isn't *bad*. You need to ask Ms. Elizabeth about that."

He pointed at the building behind us.

Remy's wolf magic whipped around faster than the man. A wide-eyed, happy head and snout moved first, followed by the ruff of his neck and his arching wolf back, bouncing legs, and wagging tail. Then

Remy himself rotated at the waist, with his shoulders and one foot moving in synchronization.

His wolf knew before the boy lifted his finger to point. And his wolf was *happy*.

Remy was in a full run before I turned around.

Green, living, organic magic flooded off the building behind us.

A dark-haired woman in a high-necked red dress leaned over the rail of the upper level walkway. The dress completely covered her arms and most of her hands. Strips of the red fabric flowed up the sides of her head into the pile of hair on top of her head.

More green magic flowed from her, and the red of her dress shifted from candy apple into a darker, deeper, wine tone.

The magic streamed, as if purposefully moving toward Remy and me.

"Portia Elizabeth!" Remy called.

She stepped back from the railing and pointed at the gate. "Remy Geroux, you need to leave!" she yelled. "Now!"

CHAPTER 15

Remy took the steps to the second-floor walkway three at a time, with me close behind.

"Slow down, Remy!" She'd told us to leave, and running into a situation with an upset magical—especially a dark magical—would likely get us hurt. Badly, too, if Remy continued to leap up like a frantic puppy.

I rounded the landing to the last half-flight of steps up to the second-floor walkway. The woman in the shifting red dress had backed against the door of one of the middle apartments. Remy stood about five feet from the top step with his hands open and out.

Green, leaves-in-water streams of magic coiled around the woman and her shifting red dress. Sweet, spring greens. Deep summer, living greens. Evergreens. Grass. Crops. Life.

"I can't help you," she said. "You need to leave."

She wore red, but she wielded *green*.

"Remy." I gripped his shoulder. He couldn't barrel into this situation.

Portia Elizabeth moved into the middle of the walkway. Behind her, the moon poked through the palms and the setting desert sun.

She might be all the greens and all the reds, but the night was oranges, yellows, and purples.

Her green magic flowed outward from her body in a specific sigil pattern. It shook and manifested more than moved, and Remy and I were suddenly in a pocket inside the pattern. None of her magic touched us, yet it flowed around our bodies.

Remy didn't take his eyes off Portia Elizabeth. "I tried to find you," he said.

She wasn't just beautiful, she was *beauty*. Not in an idealized way. Not like the exaggerated transformations of the kitsune. She was a real woman with soft breasts and real muscles under smooth-yet-textured skin. Her earthy deep-brown eyes did not shimmer beyond the green of her magic. Her nose had a slight bump, her lips a generous pout, and her hips the width needed to carry the world.

The woman standing in front of us was the abundancy of all things female.

The feel of her magic changed, and its pattern reformed. One of the new lines touched Remy.

And me.

I would never lie to Portia Elizabeth. Not because I felt compelled to tell the truth. Because telling her the truth was the correct thing to do.

"Whoa," I said, and stepped back from the line of her green magic —and the connection I felt, the trust and belief, vanished.

She didn't notice. All her attention was on Remy. "I know you've been looking for me," she said.

Remy dropped his hands. "Come home."

No small talk. No conversation or questions about her life. Just a flat-out *please come back*.

She tried to cover the emotions dancing through her eyes. She tried to hold her face still, but her cheek twitched and her lip quivered.

"Alfheim is no longer my home," she said.

Her dress whiffed when she moved, and shimmered as if made of silk. And though I knew it was red, I couldn't tell what red it was—

first candy apple, then red wine. When a shadow hit, it looked like fresh blood.

The dress was neither suggestive nor modest. A tall band of fabric covered her neck, more like a thick ribbon than a collar. The fabric skimmed across her chest and breasts, but more like armor than party clothes. Her arms were covered all the way to the back of her hands. There, too, the fabric seemed to thicken into bracers.

But yet it did not. It was still a dress, and an impossible puddle of red fabric pooled around her legs.

"It could be," Remy said.

She closed her eyes. "I work for someone." The red of her dress shifted tonality and texture again. "My work keeps me here."

Remy took a step toward Portia Elizabeth.

She raised her hands and stepped back. The green magic around us changed pattern—and vibration—again.

We weren't inside a sigil. We were in a resonance pattern.

This was not magic I recognized, nor was it magic I had learned about in my studies. This magic was almost... modern. Technological. Almost. It was still clearly magic, though, and not of mundanes.

"Who do you work for?" I asked. If Remy wasn't going to stick to basic conversation, neither would I. Because her magic might be a new threat worse than any we'd seen yet.

She pointed at me. "You were part of the dark magic that stole Anthea."

"Not my choice," I said.

Remy looked between us. "Those kids said something about Anthea being good? Is that possible? A good vampire?"

"You two need to leave. Now." She pointed at the steps.

"Portia..." Remy took another step toward her.

Her green magic tightened around him. "Heed me. Go back to your hotel, Remy Geroux. Tell Arne Odinsson I cannot help."

Remy shook as if he wanted to fight her directive, but he didn't. I knew he couldn't, because I also knew I would do exactly what she wanted me to do, not because she forced me, but because it was the correct course of action.

She was green and life and living. She was primal and perfect and our reason for walking The Land of the Living. To not do what she asked would be to allow the entropy of The Land of the Dead to win.

Yet...

Something was wrong. I couldn't pinpoint what, or how, but my instincts pulled my attention from the resonance patterns of Portia Elizabeth's magic to the apartment complex.

Its concealment enchantments were about to put up a fight.

The apartment doors wavered and flickered the way the world blanks and comes back when you're too aware of your own blinking eyelids. I closed my eyes, then opened, and did my best to focus through the troll scat.

Were we truly inside the enchantments? Were we really talking to Portia Elizabeth? The swirling blue and red lights said so, but we weren't supposed to be here. Raven didn't want us here.

I should have known better than to think a gatekeeper would simply let us in. I should have paid attention to the real make-up of the enchantment. To the shimmer in the air and the electricity dancing along my skin, and to motivations behind the concealments.

Just because the troll scat made my brain see rainbows and my skin feel the universe's tug, didn't mean any of it was real magic.

My arm extended, and my fist flicked—my body instinctively went through the motions of tossing out a tracer enchantment. A century's worth of practice with spells along my forearms was hard to break.

But my brother had stripped me of my tracers and protection enchantments. "Remy," I said.

He didn't answer.

I should have remembered what Maura said before we left: Beware the tricksters.

I looked back toward where Remy should have been standing.

Chip waved and popped a "teriyaki Chablis" potato chip into her kitsune mouth.

CHAPTER 16

I was no longer inside the apartment complex's enchantment walls. I was no longer outside at all, but back in the hallway between my hotel room and Remy's. Gravel-like, golden-green carpet whiffed against the soles of my boots. The bright glare of the halogen light overhead burned down onto my head.

I shielded my eyes.

If the kitsune had snatched me right out of the apartment complex and through an entrenched, powerful concealment enchantment, they would have had to open a gate to move me, and no such gate had happened.

Two supposedly-minor Japanese trickster spirits moved *me*, or they were messing with my head and I was still standing on the walkway in front of Portia Elizabeth's apartment door.

My money was on an illusion.

"What did you two do?" I spread out my arms as if I could keep them off me by pushing them away. "Portia Elizabeth!" I yelled. "We have a kitsune issue!"

"Troll scat will do that, Mr. Victorsson," Chip said. "It makes you sensitive to all you see."

The two kitsune leaned against the wall on either side of my door. I threw the troll scat bag at Chip's head.

She ducked. Lollipop pulled a bright yellow *tsking* emoji sucker, complete with little waving cartoon finger, out of her mouth.

"How did you get past the enchantments?" I yelled. "Where's Remy? Where's Portia Elizabeth?"

Remy was probably on his way back to the hotel. Portia Elizabeth wanted us to leave. The kitsune did me a favor, really.

No. She used her magic to influence me into thinking we needed to leave.

Lollipop rolled her eyes.

The kitsune had switched clothes. Lollipop now wore the blinding tropical shirt and Chip, the yellow polo. Chip had shifted into an anime-worthy, bouncy, super-sexualized female body with gravity-defying balloon-breasts and a waist that, though possible, was not probable on any real woman, magical or mundane.

Lollipop still appeared to be a stereotypical young tourist with bags and pockets full of devices, though the cargo shorts and the white tube socks with the sneakers seemed more American than Japanese.

"Is he safe?" They weren't going to give me a straight answer, no matter what I asked, but I had to try. "Is Portia Elizabeth safe?" What if they messed with her, too?

I pressed on my forehead. Why was I so worried about a woman I didn't know? One with major magic she used to influence me?

Because she influenced me.

Lollipop winked.

"What do you want?" I asked. "Why are we back at the hotel?"

Chip rustled her bag of potato crisps, and the label and coloring shifted from "salt and salmon" to "melon paprika."

"Why do you think you left?" She set a chip on her tongue and slurped it in like a lizard.

"I thought you two were fox spirits, not reptiles," I said.

Lollipop shifted her eyes to lizard slits, then back. She grinned and pulled a happy, cartoon gecko candy from her mouth.

Both flicked their huge, multiple fox tails.

I pointed at Remy's door. "At least tell me if my friend is safe." And *Portia Elizabeth*, I thought.

"This is not good," I said. She influenced me to heed her and now I was fixated.

Lollipop pulled from her mouth a smiling lemon-colored happy-emoji-shaped candy.

There would be no reasoning with the kitsune, nor would they tell me more information about the hows and whys of the moment than what served them. They might have an agenda. They might not. They, like the troll, might just be on vacation. They might be working for a higher-up kami. They might not.

"I don't think you two care one bit about why we're in Las Vegas." I could still expedite whatever trick they wanted to play and pull off that bandage, so to speak. They were going to mess with me no matter what, so I might as well get it over with and get back to the job Arne sent us to do.

"What do you want?" I asked again. "Spit it out. I'm busy."

Chip shrugged and bit into a "lavender marmalade" chip.

I pointed at the bag. "Could you wait until the troll scat wears off before flicking out the strange flavors?" If she flipped over to oyster-flavored anything, I'd vomit on both of them.

"Now, now, Mr. Victorsson." Chip suggestively laid a crisp on her tongue. "We have questions."

"*You* have questions? Where is Remy?" I banged on his door. "Remy!"

Lollipop wagged her finger. She frowned and pulled the chocolate wolf out of her mouth again.

"He's not going to hurt either of you!" I yelled. "Bait him. Bait me. Have your fun, but neither of us is here for you." We were here for…

I stopped the influenced thought in its tracks and pounded on his door again.

"You will answer our questions *first*," Chip said.

"Why? Where's Remy?" I pulled my phone out of my pocket. Maybe my GPS would tell me where I actually was.

Chip stepped close and looked around my arm.

I swiped open my phone's screen and looked down at a woman hugging my dog. An exceptional woman.

"*Ohhh…*" Chip pointed and grinned.

They knew something about the woman in the picture. The woman who I knew I *should* remember.

More so than Portia Elizabeth. *This* woman was why I walked The Land of the Living. Literally why I was still alive. I was sure of it.

"Who is she?" I waved the picture under their noses. "Why can't I remember her?" Why did I keep forgetting that I didn't remember her?

Chip popped a now "dark chocolate mole" chip into her mouth.

Lollipop pulled the shimmering, cartoon love-filled heart out of her mouth once again.

Maybe they were only sensing my emotions. Maybe they didn't know any more than I did and were just taunting me. "You tell me who she is."

Chip shook her head. "Information first."

Of course they wanted information. "Niklas der Nord is looking to depose Arne Odinsson. How's that?" I tucked my phone back into my pocket.

Lollipop rolled her eyes again.

Chip crinkled her snack bag. "Your brother," she said.

The creature my father built out of vampire parts? "What about him? He's a nasty piece of work."

Chip leaned closer. "He is new magic."

"No," I said. "He's reconstituted old demon-magic."

Chip and Lollipop looked at each other as if they hadn't even considered the idea.

"Look," I said, "I don't have time to mess around, no matter how fun you two might be." Because they were just as likely to derail our search as they were to point me in the right direction.

Lollipop grinned and winked. This time, when she pulled her sucker out, it was shaped like a lime-flavored heavy metal devil's horn hand sign.

I chuckled. Maybe I could reach some sort of equilibrium with them. "Why do you want information about my brother?"

They looked at each other with tightly-closed lips, then shook their heads *no*.

"If your kami bosses have a vampire problem, all they need to do is ask," I said. "Alfheim—Arne's Alfheim—will help. Not just me. We *will* help. Vampires are bad for everyone's business."

I no longer cared about the dangers of offering help to tricksters. Arne would help. Der Nord, I wasn't so sure about. Not that he could keep me from providing support to anyone fighting vampires.

They looked at me again.

But they were tricksters. I had to give them some excuse to be naughty. "As long as you promise to leave Remy alone." He could handle two kitsune, but it would be nice to not have the distraction. "*And* tell me what you know about the woman in the picture. You do both, or no help."

Chip frowned. Lollipop pulled out a purple snarling pit bull sucker wearing a spiky collar.

"I know you don't like dogs, and dogs don't like you, but Remy's a werewolf. He's a man. He's not going to hurt you." I nodded toward his door. "He's much more angry at the elves downstairs than he is at you, anyway."

They flicked their magical tails and looked at each other again. "We must promise, Mister Huge and New?"

"Yes," I said. "Don't be skittish around him. His wolf finds skittish *very* interesting, and even though he won't hurt you, he might slap a paw on your throat just for good measure."

They both nodded.

"Good," I said. "First, tell me the truth about where we are. Talk."

Chip popped a "wasabi chipotle" chip into her mouth. Lollipop continued to suck on her candy.

I shook my head and pulled out my phone again. Perhaps now they would give me information on the woman in the photo. "Why did you two—"

Lollipop snatched my phone. She twisted away, and danced down the hallway while holding the phone against her cheek.

"Hey!" I yelled. Goddamned tricksters. "Give that back!"

I looked down at Chip.

She'd transformed into the woman in the photo. Same face. Same eyes. Same clothes. "Frank," she said. "I miss you."

The best way to deal with tricksters was to not let them get under your skin, and to allow their taunts and jabs to roll off your back. Which, honestly, was one of the key lessons tricksters taught unsuspecting mundanes—don't let the fools get to you.

The other lesson was to never take a situation for granted, and to always know that no matter how much you think you understand the context of an event, you really know nothing at all.

Maybe Chip mimicking the woman in the photo was the exact cut they needed to breach the surface of my skin. Maybe the mental gymnastics necessary to ignore the perceptual lack-of-context of the moment had frayed my nerves. Maybe it was the troll scat.

I didn't know and I didn't care.

All the exasperated calm I'd felt when I realized I wasn't inside the apartment complex—or I was, and in the middle of a trickster mind game—burst like a balloon.

I bellowed and swiped at Chip's head. She snickered and ran down the hallway after Lollipop. "You want my help?" I yelled.

They ran around a corner. Lollipop stopped long enough to blow me a kiss.

"Give me back my phone, you two obnoxious little—"

I skidded around the corner—and directly into an alcove at the end of the apartment building's walkway. A palm tree rustled just off the railing. Crickets chirped, but no one shouted from the pool. The air held the same night-in-the-desert chill it had when we'd landed.

Deep night and stars shimmered in the sky.

I'd lost *hours*.

What was going on? Was this yet another illusion? I backed out of the alcove. I'd bang on every door in the complex to get answers if I had to.

I rounded the corner onto the walkway—and pulled up short directly in front of Raven.

She still wore her hair in low braids, but this time, she also wore a black knit stocking cap, a black leather biker jacket, jeans, a white t-shirt, and a pair of big, tall, black boots.

Her magic flared and spread behind her like two massive wings unable to fully unfold in the apartment's walkway. Feathers rustled. A breeze hit my face. And Raven smiled up at me.

"Mr. Victorsson," she said. "Kitsune are downright naughty, aren't they?" She tapped her finger against her chin.

"I need my phone." My flare of rage, thankfully, had depleted itself once the kitsune were out of visual range.

Raven laughed. "Kitsune *do* enjoy a lonely man."

I scowled. Damned tricksters.

"You do not wear your heart on your sleeve, Mr. Victorsson." She swirled her finger at my chin. "You wear it on your face. I'd stay away from the poker tables, if I were you."

She wanted to chitchat? "What, exactly, is going on here?"

She grabbed my chin and twisted my head to look at my Yggdrasil tattoo. "The elves do quality work," she said. "The Tree of Life suits you."

She wasn't going to answer my questions. She probably wouldn't answer any questions about anything unless that answer funneled me toward whatever lesson she believed I needed to learn, because that's what tricksters did. They got their jollies from teaching the unsuspecting "lessons."

"Please let go of my face," I said.

Her fingers lifted off my chin and she held up her hands as if to signal "no harm."

Her wings spread again. Iridescent greens and purples played along the feathers. Clouds of sparks rose. And just as quickly, she pulled them back into whatever pocket she kept them.

"So it's true. You see magic beyond what the scat is showing you." She looked me over as if expecting to see my own personal spellwork. "Valuable."

"Do you know how I can get my phone back from the kitsune?" I asked. I had to try.

"Do you wish to make a deal, Mr. Victorsson?"

We already had a "deal," one that I suspected would not turn out well for me in the long run.

Raven swirled her finger under my chin. "I have traded your offer of services, Mr. Victorsson. This deal would be new, and between us."

My chest and throat tightened. What did she do? "Traded my services? What does that mean?" Was I about to get my head ripped off by some other trickster? I glanced over my shoulder at the black night beyond the apartment building's balcony.

Maybe I had a bargaining chip. "My offer of services was non-transferable," I said. Not that it mattered with tricksters.

Raven laughed. "Well, I guess I'll just need to ask for it back." She winked.

Harm was coming my way. A big harm or a little harm, I did not know, but the trickster in front of me was manipulating me toward something bad.

"No new deal," I said anyway. "Not with you."

Raven tapped my chest. "You worry too much. If I were a god of death, I would have dealt with the problem that is you already, Mr. Victorsson."

No, Raven was often depicted in Native American myths as a creator. "Your job has always been to tempt the fearful out of their shells." Sending harm my way fit with the "drive them out of their comfort zone" aspect of her spirit.

Raven laughed. "Because I'm *bored*, Mr. Victorsson. Do you have any idea how mind-numbingly dull the daily routines of mundanes are? There is very little knowledge and memory to collect there."

Knowledge. Memory. Had I been wrong? Was Raven not a native spirit?

Raven grinned. "The world has new ways." She tapped my chest. "New methods for building gods."

Was I in the presence of a full-fledged *god* and not a tradition-specific spirit? Nor was she an elf, kami, or fae who had come to take on the aspects of a god.

She laughed again. "That troll scat makes you see things you should not. It's quite a tool, isn't it?"

A trickster *god* was messing with me because she was bored. "You're interfering," I said. "On purpose. Because you think I'm *routinely* setting about finding answers." She had zero information. Zero actual connection to anything—not the woman in the picture on my phone. Not Portia Elizabeth, no matter how she played that she did. Most definitely not the elves, and probably not the kitsune, no matter how entertaining those two would be at a party.

Was Raven here, standing in my way, simply because I was the shiny thing that fell out of the elves' pocket? All her talk of deals suggested she was more interested in playing than in helping.

Raven pouted. "Your expression wounds me, Mr. Victorsson."

"I don't have time for games. Yours or anyone else's."

"In Las Vegas?" Raven snorted. "That's like saying you buy Playboy for the articles."

No more chitchat. Not with this trickster. "I need my phone," I said. "Portia Elizabeth is a succubus and she influenced us. I need to know if Remy's okay."

Raven's features hardened—literally took on a muscle tension that flattened the planes around her eyes and hollowed out her cheeks. "Do not use derogatory terms, Mr. Victorsson."

Derogatory?

Of course *succubus* was derogatory. How could it not be? Remy even said they didn't know for sure what kind of spirit Portia Elizabeth was.

I was an idiot. "I apologize," I said. I'd just pissed off the trickster to whom I had previously offered help—and I couldn't shake the feeling I was about to pay for my transgressions.

"Yes. You do." She raised her hand high above her head.

And Raven, the trickster—or perhaps the creator—snapped her fingers against my forehead.

CHAPTER 17

Portia Elizabeth leaned over me. She gripped my chin and pressed her fingers into my jaw. "Why are we doing this, Raven?" she said.

We were in the back of an SUV. Not our rental SUV—a different one upholstered in gray fabric. I was crammed in diagonally with my head on the flat rear seats next to the back of the front passenger seat. Portia Elizabeth sat cross-legged to my side. Raven, with her wings there-but-not, drove.

Portia Elizabeth's red dress shifted and her green magic resonated. Behind her, through the window, yellow streetlights flickered by.

"Because he's a shiny, new bauble who offered his services." Raven glanced over her shoulder. "The elves sent hounds into my territory. Of course I'm going to adopt the big, friendly one."

"I can handle it myself, Raven. You didn't have to—"

"He *offered*," Raven said. "And he's big enough to get the job done."

I groaned.

"He works for *Alfheim*," Portia Elizabeth said.

Raven laughed. "Yes," she said. "Yes, he does."

Portia Elizabeth inhaled, then slowly exhaled as she checked my eyes. "I think he's coming around."

Raven took a left onto another road. "Not too much, I hope."

Portia Elizabeth laid her hand on my forehead. "He's cold. What if he carries an unseen elven enchantment? Maybe your magic reacted adversely."

Raven signaled and took a left onto another street. "He's not carrying protection spells or tracer enchantments. I checked. You know we couldn't take him in if he carried tracers."

Portia Elizabeth leaned back. "I sent Remy back to the hotel. We should send Victorsson back, too. You know this isn't right, Raven."

"But it is necessary."

Portia Elizabeth leaned over me again. "Why didn't you follow Remy?"

"The kitsune stole my phone," I mumbled. "They interfered."

I knew, once again, that I would never lie to Portia Elizabeth. Not because I felt compelled to tell the truth. Because telling her the truth was the correct thing to do. "And I'm always cold when I wake up."

She touched my forehead and cheeks, and frowned like a mother checking for a fever.

I still couldn't tell what red her dress was—under one flickering streetlight, it looked like wet brick. Under the next, red cotton candy. When a shadow hit, like port.

"Did you know about the kitsune?" she asked Raven. "A few of them can cast and alter powerful illusions. Concealment enchantments have no effect on them."

The SUV pulled up to a light. "I knew about the kitsune," Raven said. "Ask him why they're so interested in him."

Portia Elizabeth frowned, but her green magic resonance shifted into a new shape. "What do they want?"

"They wanted information about vampires."

Raven frowned over her shoulder before taking the SUV through the intersection.

"We need to take him back to his hotel," Portia Elizabeth said.

"He offered his services," Raven said. "Didn't you, Mr. Victorsson?"

"Raven said she traded them." No use lying about it. Not that I could, anyway.

"You shouldn't have done that," Portia Elizabeth said. She looked up at Raven. "I damned well hope you get something good out of this exchange."

Raven shrugged.

"You could use that resonant magic of yours and make me never offer help to anyone ever again." Maybe I'd get something good out of this situation.

Portia Elizabeth frowned. "I work hard at holding my dark tendencies in check, Mr. Victorsson."

I'd offended her. "I apologize. I didn't mean…" I trailed off and set my head back down onto the SUV's rough upholstery. Every word that came out of my mouth with Portia Elizabeth seemed to make matters worse.

A rapport, we did not have.

We took a left. "He sees magic," Raven said. "Anthea hadn't finished the job when she vanished." She glanced back. "The last thing this world needs is you fighting."

Portia Elizabeth inhaled and slowly exhaled again, as if doing a calming exercise.

"Where are you taking me?" Outside, the streetlights grew farther apart. "I have work in Alfheim. I can't replace your Anthea." No matter how well I could fight.

I tried to sit up, but Portia Elizabeth ran the back of her hand—and its smooth, cool, red silk—across the Yggdrasil tattoo on the side of my head.

"Hush," she said.

"Okay." No more questions, at least for now, but I'd still explain every happen- and circumstance to Portia Elizabeth the moment she asked.

Her eyes narrowed and she glanced down and to the side as if listening to someone. Then she sniffed at the skin of my forearm. "You wore protection spells for several decades," she said.

"Dracula stole my spells and my tracer enchantments." I held up my forearms for her to see.

"Dracula?" Portia Elizabeth looked up at Raven. "*Dracula* opened the portals?"

"Why do you think Anthea couldn't resist?" Raven answered.

Portia Elizabeth stroked my skin. "The Lord of the Vampires messed with you, didn't he?"

I nodded.

She did her inhale-exhale again. "I do not recognize the elf responsible for your tracers."

"Dagrun Tyrsdottir," I said.

Portia Elizabeth touched my cheek and a small smile appeared on her full, lovely mouth. "I was gone from Alfheim before the Icelandic elves came to town," she said.

"Remy told me."

A tendril of her mahogany-black hair slid from the bun on her head and slid across my cheek when she checked my eyes again. I swore for a split-second, her lip quivered. But she caught her body's display of emotion and stopped it in its tracks.

"He showed me the portraits he drew of you. He keeps them in an enchanted pouch so they don't fade away."

Raven threw me a look that was part *you're adorable*, and part *you poor thing*. Where Portia Elizabeth showed a motherly side, Raven showed bemused aunt.

I tried to sit up again, but Portia Elizabeth put her hand on my chest. She stared at the back of the seats, then shook her head as if deciding not to pursue more questions about Remy. "Tell me about Alfheim," she said.

I'd tell her the entire detailed history, if she wanted. "I came to town two centuries ago. Arne took me in. He took in Rose, too, when I returned with her on my hip from fighting in the Civil War. He took her in even though she was a witch," I said. "He took in two vampires. They lasted seventy years before they turned on us. One turned out to be Radu the Handsome, the younger brother of Vlad the Impaler."

"And Arne still allowed them to live in town?" Portia Elizabeth asked. "Even after the havoc I caused?"

"Yes," I said. "He says dark magicals can move to neutral if they're offered a worthwhile opportunity to do so. He doesn't expect friendship, or even trust, but diplomatic associations. He needs you to look all the other elves in the eye and tell them that taking a chance at diplomacy with a dark magical is worth the effort. Show them how you've changed and held onto those changes these three centuries."

"What about Remy and Gerard?" She lifted her hand off my chest. "Why can't they stand at the Conclave?"

"Remy will. I will. We're witnesses. But Arne's certain that you have something special to say. Something the other elves need to hear."

"The kings are male, Mr. Victorsson," Portia Elizabeth said. "And I would guess that the majority of the entourages will also be male."

I hadn't considered that Arne wanted Portia Elizabeth there because she was a spirit labeled succubus. "Maybe he's counting on your abilities to cut through their bluster and table-banging. Plus the queens will be there, too, including Dagrun."

Portia Elizabeth laughed. "Tell me, Frank Victorsson, do you truly believe that the Elf Queens would not use my presence to their advantage?"

Dag would use her presence to the advantage of all elves, not just herself and her husband.

"There's a usurper. His name is Niklas der Nord. He'll destroy Alfheim. The Alfheim Pack has more than thirty members. Remy, Gerard, and Axlam have helped countless wolves since you left," I said. "Niklas der Nord will declare them dark and evict the pack."

She glanced toward Raven as if expecting an admonishment for asking questions. "Axlam?"

"Gerard's wife," I said. "She came to us in the early nineties. She was attacked by a werewolf in a refugee camp. She's everything the wolves can be. She's the first of the pack to get a college degree after being turned."

I swear a tear appeared at the corner of Portia Elizabeth's eye. She shook it off. "Does Remy have someone?" She glanced at Raven again, then leaned closer. "What did he say about me?" she whispered.

Raven's semi-present wings fluttered.

Portia Elizabeth sat up and all the emotion her body had shown vanished once again. "I am no longer part of Alfheim, Mr. Victorsson," she said.

"We need your help." No lying. No dancing around needs, either.

Portia Elizabeth returned her hand to my chest. "This is not my fight. I cannot intervene in elven politics."

She spread her silk-covered fingers directly over my heart. I tried harder to sit up, but somehow she held me down.

"Stay down," she said.

I couldn't fight her. I would never fight this woman, though I would fight *for* her, so I would be worthy of her touches.

All that pooled red fabric didn't hide the truth—Portia Elizabeth was the balance to all the storms. She was the fortress at the center of the world, the one place we were all safe, healthy, and fed.

"What *are* you?" I asked.

She shook her head. She wasn't going to tell me.

I pushed against Portia Elizabeth's hand. "Please." I wouldn't be the bull in their china shop. I wouldn't sow discord or domination or ill manners. But I needed answers.

Portia Elizabeth lifted away her hand.

I sat up. We were off the Strip and driving toward the massive isolated glass boxes on the edge of town. Shiny things moved by outside. Interesting things. Things made of metal, chrome, neon, glass. Things a raven might like.

Not one of the buildings we drove by had been here in the early sixties, when I was robbed by a showgirl. The Strip had been completely gutted and rebuilt since then. Most of the houses out on the edge had, as well. Every building in Vegas taller than three stories had to be no more than a quarter-century old.

Maybe that was why Las Vegas attracted magicals and conclaves. The city wove itself a shiny new glamour every few decades.

Portia Elizabeth gathered her dress's flowing red fabric. It puffed and whiffed, and no obvious changes occurred, but it ceased to be just a dress.

She now wore leggings under her skirt—leggings that appeared as armored as the sleeves of her top. Every time Portia Elizabeth moved, her red dress became less dress-like. It continued to shimmer and flow like silk, and continued to refuse to settle on one red, but the sense it gave off was less formalwear and more combat-wear.

But she didn't look ready to fight, nor did her green magic. She looked agitated. "No more questions," she said.

I bowed my head. If she wished me silent, I would stay silent.

Raven drove, and occasionally glanced at Portia Elizabeth, or at me. We passed three huge buildings that could have either been more casinos or some sort of corporate offices, and ended up on a lonely two-lane road out of the city. Palm trees lined the road, first only a few hundred feet apart, then every quarter mile, before giving way to cacti.

Odd cacti—huge barrel cactuses that looked to be taller than me. Saguaros that towered like the hotels back in Vegas. Saguaros that should not be in Nevada.

"When did we enter Arizona?" I asked. And not northern Arizona. The saguaro was native to the southwestern corner of the state.

I'd forgotten to stay quiet.

Portia Elizabeth patted my hand. Her dress had fully transformed into a full-body red fight-suit in a style I did not recognize. The fabric had migrated up her neck to her hairline behind her ears. Only her face, hair, and fingers remained uncovered, and like the variability of its red hue, its fit—tight, loose, formfitting, open—oscillated as well.

And part of me wondered if it was speaking to her.

"I have an elven axe," I said. "She chose me. She talks to me, but not really *talk*. She skips the words part and makes me understand her meaning."

Portia Elizabeth smiled. "I like you."

I smiled back. "Seems I'm likable."

Both Portia Elizabeth and Raven laughed.

"Odinsson was right to take you in," Raven said.

"He takes a lot of us in," I said. "That's why he needs our help."

Portia Elizabeth touched my cheek, but did not respond. Instead, she reached past me and rolled down the window.

Cool twilight air swept over my head and shoulders. The sun out here hung just at the edge of the mountains, which ringed us on all sides. We were inside a bowl—a magnificent world-bowl, one full of the sweet-savory scent of desert sage and the thinly-golden taste of prickly-pear. This was a place that did not need syrupy sweetness. It did not need maples or honeybees. It needed its saguaros and tarantulas.

We'd driven into another realm.

The last evening rays hit the desert dust and the sky burst in bright salmons, reds, oranges, purples, and hints of greens and blues. The colors shimmered much like the aurora borealis, but they didn't waver or fall in sheets. Out here, they were the sky, and the sky was them. The aurora had exploded into the heavens and we drove inside the remains of its rainbow corpse.

The road ceased its modern concrete smoothness and took on its original horse-trail gravel.

Raven pointed down the gravel path to an intersection. A spot at which the path we followed intersected not one, but two other paths, at angles I could not fathom. Angles that made no sense, but were there, in front of the SUV, converging in a magical space that had to be offset from reality.

Offset like the space around The Great Hall at home. Offset like Rose's borderland, but not as much as the pocket in which the elves locked Dracula and his minions.

A sign manifested out of the shimmering multi-colored sky. An odd sign. A sign that had no place outside anyone's Great Hall.

Metal hoops swung around the central glowing orb. The first hoop sat at a forty-five-degree angle to the pole supporting the sign, and another hoop, also at a forty-five-degree angle to the first hoop, attached to the first at a single point. The structure rotated on the pole and created the optical illusion of electrons circling an atomic nucleus.

Crossroads Saloon, it said in a blocky, kitschy, sixties font.

"We *are* in Nevada," Portia Elizabeth said.

Nevada. Non-Nevadan, Sonoran Desert plants. Technology.

Magic. Someone had built a restaurant at an intersection at the edge of many worlds.

Raven and Portia Elizabeth had brought me to a literal and metaphorical crossroads.

Raven pulled into the empty—but not empty—parking lot. I couldn't see any other vehicles. I felt them, though. A sense of *chariots* filled the flat hard-packed desert around the building.

New chariots. Old chariots. Natural and magical, technological and fantastic.

I stepped out and looked up at the sky. Magic shimmered as if just out of reach. It swirled like fairy lights around the boards, clear doors, and windows of the Crossroads Saloon.

A pounding bass rolled out of the building. The air smelled of grilled meats and roasted root vegetables. The entire interior seemed to be visible from outside, yet it clearly was not. There were magicals in there. Magicals of types I suspected I'd never met before, and likely never would again.

"Best food on the planet," Raven said. She straightened her knit cap. "One could argue that the Crossroads outside of Tokyo serves better fish." She leaned against the fender of our SUV chariot. "The Crossroads in Alice Springs serves lizard, though the one in Germany has the best beer."

"How many Crossroads are there?" I asked.

She pointed over her shoulder. "Planet-wide? Don't know."

Portia Elizabeth shrugged. "There are two more marked locations in North America. One is in the Sonoma Valley outside San Francisco."

Something about this exchange picked at the bottom of my brain.

Portia Elizabeth stared at my chest as if my heart was whispering its own incantation. Her eyes narrowed, and her green energy contracted into a shimmering, flowing wave of energy not all that different from what her dress had looked like when I woke up.

Raven didn't seem to notice, or if she did, opening the doors took all her attention and she'd decided to ignore us.

Her wings fully manifested in the air over our heads, spread in the clear raven gliding position. No angel wings here. Raven was all that was *raven* in the world—all the cunning perception. All the precise attention. And every ounce of the cleverness of the corvids.

But she was more than the intelligent, bored trickster. I was in the presence of the best of what plucked out a living under the shadow of fighting giants. Raven was the wisdom necessary to avoid being trampled. She was the knowledge needed to feed oneself and one's family after the predators have decimated and reformed an ecosystem. She was cunning. She was the refusal to lie down and die.

Raven was the shrewdness that manifests within an abundant system. She wasn't just a god. She was adaptability.

I was in the presence of one of the primordial forces of evolution.

Raven, this spirit I had associated with North America, was much more—she was native, but she was also native to the world.

She winked.

Portia Elizabeth curled her hand around my elbow and...

We moved.

CHAPTER 18

The open serving floor of the Crossroads Saloon was
significantly larger than the exterior of the building should
have allowed—even though it wasn't. What felt like hundreds of tables
spread out before me—table after table in a massive, grand Hall—
though I only saw perhaps twenty, and they fully occupied the space I
perceived.

I closed my eyes, blinked, then looked again. A performance area
filled the wall directly ahead of me, and appeared close enough that I
clearly could see the lonely stage with an old upright piano.

I twisted my head and listened, and yes, under the din of restaurant chatter, a soft, sweet piano tune filtered through the room. I
couldn't place it—or hold it in memory long enough to think about
the notes—but it wafted through the air on the back of the scents of
grilling meats and beer.

To the right, another wall with several doors leading to what was
likely the kitchen, private rooms, etc. To the left, a huge thirty-foot
carved wood bar backed by an equally huge mirror. Closer to the
stage sat another section with raised booths, shielded by curtains of
magic.

I blinked again. The walls were too close. No way should *hundreds* of tables fit inside, yet they did. They were here. I knew they were here. I just couldn't perceive them.

Of the tables I did see, shadows shimmered as if physical and reflective in the low light, and hid each table's occupants.

I must be looking at layer upon layer of glamours. Individual glamours, room glamours, building glamours all embedded inside a huge crossroads glamour that distorted space and time the same way as the glamour around The Great Hall.

Portia Elizabeth stood to my left. She placed her hand on my arm and nodded into the saloon. "Come," she said.

Raven was nowhere to be seen.

"How come I've never heard of this place?" We wove between shadowed, slippery tables. "I study," I said. When your daughter is a witch, it's the smart thing to do. "This place doesn't feel like a border-land between The Lands of the Living and the Dead."

We moved around another table but still hadn't moved any perceivable distance into the room. "I'd think the elves would be well aware of any place with so many glamours."

Portia Elizabeth stopped in a gap between tables and reached for my hand. I let her take it.

"Wolf will explain," she said. But mostly I got the impression I was asking too many questions.

The glamour around The Great Hall had a dazzle to it—a bit of shock and awe that overwhelmed and dissuaded questions. Cross-roads Saloon had the same sort of nimble brilliance, as if the spell-work itself did not want a questioner to figure out and exploit its flaws. Which, if anything, told me I was inside a grand magic. One that, like The Great Hall, had not been built by just a single wielder, but was a magnificent spellwork structure born from the work and power of many talented beings.

Beings who surrounded me as they laughed and dined behind their personal glamours.

What had Raven and Portia Elizabeth pulled me into? Had I unwittingly allowed myself to be dragged into enemy territory?

Portia Elizabeth gripped my hand. "Stop worrying. Keep your wits about you," she said.

You're not paranoid if everyone really is out to get you, I thought, but she wanted me to stop with such thoughts, so I did.

We walked around table after table and magicks after magicks. Some tables felt as if spirits partied, some as if dark, angry things dined. A few felt familiar, as if touched by witches. But none felt elven —or fae.

Portia Elizabeth tugged on my hand. "Watch your step."

We'd come to the raised area to the side of the bar. Golden railings covered with shifting, rotating sigils separated it from the main floor. Sheets of distortion hung from the ceiling. I picked out booths in the shadows, but nothing else.

Portia Elizabeth led me up the single step into the special section.

Anubis sat in the booth directly across from the step. A lovely meal of fragrant roasted meat, root vegetables, and unleavened bread filled the table. The god winked his jackal eye and raised his beer as we passed by.

"Was that—"

Portia Elizabeth shook her head. "You cannot be star-struck, Frank Victorsson. Not when meeting Wolf."

Star-struck meant not thinking straight, and she obviously wanted me on my best game.

Laughter rolled out of the shadows in the next booth. The one after that held seven spirits I did not recognize. They, too, raised their beers to us.

The final booth, the one closest to the stage, shimmered with a light all its own. Someone laughed. A yip followed, then a growl. A denim-wearing leg and a big, black boot dropped out of the side.

Raven stepped out of the booth into the space directly in front of Portia Elizabeth. She waved me forward.

Sitting in the center of the booth, one arm draped along the back of the maroon leather and the other flipping a fork between his— hers? I couldn't tell—fingers, had to be the spirit they called Wolf.

The spirit sat, but we looked each other directly in the eye.

Gunmetal gray hair stood straight up from the spirit's head and added to its height. Ice blue eyes stared at me from sharp, angular features. Coiled muscles worked under a smooth, clinging, gray silk shirt, and tensed along an exquisite long neck.

Magic danced around the spirit, but not like the winged magic that so clearly marked Raven.

This spirit's magic danced and yipped. It prowled and it played. It formed one node, then another, then another, as if moving from one member of a pack to another.

I bowed my head courteously. "Wolf," I said. "Greetings."

It sniffed. The hand on the back of the booth dropped below the table and a new yip followed.

Pup ears appeared, then a snout, though this "pup" had to be full adult-timber-wolf-size not to have completely vanished next to the spirit.

The snout and ears dropped below the lip of the table.

This was not a Native American spirit, in much the same world-essence way that Raven was not a singular spirit from any specific indigenous tradition. Was I in the presence of *the* Wolf, the essence of all the versions of Wolf who populated all of the world's magicks? This Wolf carried predatory might. Every single wolf- and dog-like ability to hunt, herd, and control what needed hunting, herding, and controlling all but shimmered in the air around it.

But this Wolf lacked a strong sense of pack. Power oozed from this semi-world-spirit on a level I did not think possible, but it was not all that was the World Wolf. No, this Wolf was more Las Vegas than it was world.

I was in the presence of an *urban* spirit.

Wolf rubbed the tip of its nose and peered at me as if reading every one of my stray twitches as a threat.

The spirit tilted its head. It cupped one elbow with a hand, then tapped the fingers of the other against its cheek.

It grinned.

I understood vulnerability. I came into this world a lumbering mountain of naïve pain. But never in my life have I felt so blatantly stalked.

If Wolf wished to take me down, there would be no escape, no matter how I fought or ran.

"Do you understand where you are, Mr. Victorsson?" it asked.

I damned well better not show fear. "No," I said. Or lie.

It frowned. "Do you understand *what* this place is?"

It'd kill me if I answered wrong. It would rip off bits, gnaw me to the bone, and leave me in the identical state from which my father plucked me. "A Great Hall." I had no idea what else to call it.

Wolf nodded. "Close enough."

I exhaled. I had no idea I'd been holding my breath.

It leaned against the back of its booth. "So you're the giant?"

The question caught me off guard. "I'm not a jotunn," I said. "It's a nickname the elves use." Like "Biterson" for the vampires, but I didn't say that to Wolf.

Wolf laughed. "Yes, yes." Wolf winked. "Now I understand why Raven finds you interesting."

She'd vanished. Portia Elizabeth still stood to my side, but Raven was gone.

Wolf's magic flickered in the corner of my eye, demanding I bolt away and directly into its pack member waiting on my other side. It was playing with its food.

Every line of Wolf's mouth, nose, and eyes accentuated. The shadows of its cheeks darkened, but its eyes brightened. "Why are you in my territory, Mr. Victorsson?"

I was pretty sure that the entire planet was some Wolf or another's territory, though I'd now met not one but two World and semi-World-level spirits claiming Las Vegas as theirs. Perhaps the transient —and international—nature of the city, combined with the strong, heady natural magic of the desert, made this place perfect for a powerful urban spirit to reside.

Or perhaps Wolf, like Raven, liked shiny baubles, and nothing beat Vegas in both shininess and blingy baubles.

"The Elf King of Alfheim wishes Portia Elizabeth's help," I said.

Wolf sniffed. "An elf desires help? From a succubus?" It drawled *succubus* out into an ironic string of individual phonemes.

"He asks only that she talk to the Courts." It wasn't the taking in of the dark magicals that was the problem; it was their falling off the wagon, so to speak, and Portia Elizabeth proved that a return to darkness was not inevitable.

Or so I hoped. Guessed, actually. Nothing about her green magic carried the vicious oiliness of the vampires, and the dress...

The dress was something new. Or old. I picked up nothing from it other than it was strong magic.

Magic Raven did not want Portia Elizabeth to use in a fight. I glanced back at Wolf.

I was standing in front of the unavoidable harm my offer of service was destined to drop onto my head.

Wolf must be the spirit with whom Raven made her deal.

"You are a dark magical, Portia Elizabeth?" Wolf wisped its hand in her direction.

She did not respond.

Wolf sniffed again. "My pups are not enough darkness for your elves?" it asked me.

I stood perfectly still. Wolf was not Brother, nor was it Dracula. Wolf would not be manipulated and distracted. Wolf would not make a mistake if it attacked.

"Remy Geroux will also stand as a witness," I said.

"Your elves meddle." A low growl followed. "My wolves are less wolf because of the elves."

This wolf was claiming the werewolves as its own. But how could an urban, Vegas wolf claim magicals that had been with humanity for as long as there had been humans?

A second "pup" lifted its head over the edge of the table and sniffed at the air.

I would not show fear. "Less wolf. More human," I said. I'd have a word with Remy about this. "Best for the modern world."

Wolf laughed again. "Adapt or die. Correct, Mr. Victorsson?"

I nodded. "Yes."

Wolf took a bite of its meal. It chewed steadily, its eyes on me the entire time as if I was about to steal its treats. When it swallowed, it dropped a scrap onto the floor.

Whimpering and shuffling followed, as did a few low growls.

"Your witch daughter killed an elf, did she not?" Wolf asked.

Rose, I thought. "When the witch in her became too much, yes, she did kill an elf. They were trying to help her. She didn't mean to do it."

Wolf sneered. "Your father created a new body from the parts of vampires. That body came calling, did it not?"

"It did," I said. Denying the obvious would help no one. Not me. Not the elves. Not Alfheim. "It took decades before Rose became a problem. Decades before the vampires turned on Alfheim."

Wolf sat back and placed its hand on the top of the booth's seat again. It tapped its finger and wiggled its nose. "Seems to me, Mr. Victorsson, that *you* are the core of Arne Odinsson's dark magical problem."

How was I supposed to answer such a statement?

It dropped its fork and pointed at Portia Elizabeth. "He offered his services?" it asked.

She bowed her head. "I don't believe he understood the gravity of his words."

Wolf sneered again. "Yet he offered."

She continued to look at the floor.

I dared not point out that I had offered to Raven, and that its deal was with her, not me. If I did, I had no doubt that it would shred me before I got the last word out of my mouth.

"What do you expect of me?" What did this giant spirit, this semi-god-thing that controlled so much, want with me? I was insignificant in a world brimming with magicals.

All I had was my offer of service. All I could give to any of the significantly-more-powerful elves who had adopted me—who'd helped me find my way into a livable, tolerable future—was to be the immovable mountain between them and things much worse.

Nothing else. Nothing more. I was the re-animated corpse who could take a blow, so that's what I did.

I took blows.

And now a spirit wanted to use that against me.

"You see magic, do you not, Mr. Victorsson?"

"Yes," I said. "I see pack magic around you." The roiling stalking. The hunting lunges. The need to protect. "I see meta-pack magic, as if the magic of the packs is acting like its own pack."

Wolf nodded as it approved.

"Your vampires opened gates," it said. "One opened into Las Vegas."

I'd gathered as much from the conversations at the apartment complex. "We had no control over from where Dracula pulled his army."

Wolf waved its hand as if dismissing not just my comment, but Dracula in general. "I lost Anthea to his call."

Anthea the vampire—and Portia Elizabeth—worked for Wolf. What that meant, I did not understand, but I got the feeling I'd know soon enough. "I got a pike through my chest." If Wolf was going to harm me in some way, it needed to know I could take the hit.

Wolf grinned. "You will finish the job she started." It scratched the head of one of its pups. "Bring me the troll."

I stepped back from the booth. "Why?" What did the troll do to Wolf? "We found the troll within hours of landing in Las Vegas. She's not hard to locate."

Wolf sniffed and nodded to Portia Elizabeth. "That troll owes me."

Portia Elizabeth stepped closer. "Finding her isn't the problem. She's female. Securing her cooperation has been difficult."

So the troll was uncooperative. A gambling debt seemed most likely, but with magicals it could be something as simple as a perceived slight during an introduction. The troll most likely didn't care one bit what Wolf thought, or what she might owe the spirit, and being a troll, was pretty much impervious to just about everything.

If I could spend my time gambling and ignoring a wolf-spirit crime boss, I would, too.

Portia Elizabeth touched my arm. "Hold still or this will hurt."

"What are you doing?" I should have pulled away, but her green magic changed again and she wanted me to hold still.

She cupped her hand as if holding a ball. The magic of her dress flickered and a small, writhing sphere of red *something* appeared over her palm. Too solid to be energy yet too chaotic to be solid, it wiggled and poked and danced. Its red shifted from fire-orange to apple to blood, then back. It slithered, yet did not move. It collected, yet tossed all to the wind.

I was looking at liquid magic—concentrated, intensified, physical magic.

"Take your treat," Wolf growled.

"I do not agree to this." Could I run? Would I make it out of Crossroads Saloon alive if I did? What was the red magic?

But Portia Elizabeth wanted me to hold still. "We have to, Frank," she said.

Wolf motioned at Portia Elizabeth. The resonance of her green magic shifted higher. A new pattern formed around me, one stronger and more complex than any she'd touched me with yet, and...

I stepped forward. The pup nipped at me again, but it did not matter. Only accepting Portia Elizabeth's gift mattered.

I extended my arm, fist closed and forearm up.

Wolf leaned toward me over its meal, nose forward, and sniffed at my arms. "Good boy," it said.

Portia Elizabeth slapped the red magic onto my skin.

The magic roiled and shimmered. It pushed and pulled, and pooled into a quarter-sized, unknown-red dot on my forearm.

A dot that grabbed onto my skin directly over one of the locations where my Dagrun-gifted tracer tattoos used to sit.

"Bring the troll to House," Wolf said. "You have until Thursday evening."

House must be the apartment complex, which wasn't the issue. Thursday was the beginning of the Conclave. "I have other work—"

"Your elven nonsense does not concern me, giant." Wolf wiped its fingers on its napkin. "You will provide your offered services, or you will become a pup's meal." It twitched a nostril in a very crime boss way.

Either I dragged the old lady troll to the apartment complex by Thursday evening, or the Wolf spirit in charge of Las Vegas would have me chopped up for its version of "swimmin' with the fishes."

Wolf dabbed its lips. "Do not attempt to remove your mark. If you do, Portia Elizabeth will know. Do not leave Las Vegas until your work is done." One of Wolf's pups sniffed at the tabletop. Wolf pushed it down. "Then we will discuss whether your offer of service has been fulfilled."

Portia Elizabeth's green magic swirled. I *had* to agree. I had no other choice.

"Yes," I responded.

"I am glad you understand," Wolf picked up the fork again and twirled it between its fingers. "The world is ever-changing." It pushed at the meat on its plate. "The mundanes rub against magic differently now. New powers rise and the old must respond."

It took a new bite of its meal and chewed, again staring at me as if I was about to snatch its food. "Out into the gray sky they shall go, so that the new may take their place." Then it waved at the wider universe.

I opened my mouth to respond, but Portia Elizabeth touched my arm.

"Take him back to his hotel." Wolf returned to its meal.

The pups jumped up onto the table.

They were bigger than Gerard and Remy were when in wolf form —I looked at their chests and they looked down at the top of my head —but they weren't werewolves. They weren't like any wolves I'd ever seen before.

The one on the left growled down at me with flat eyes full of fear. The one on the right, eyes full of hunger. Both had massive thick black ruffs more like lion manes than any fur I'd seen on a canine. Both were gunmetal gray and bared wicked, sharp, long teeth. Both growled. But they were not the same.

The fearful wolf carried simplistic—not simple—magic. Nothing elegant. It twisted and contorted around the wolf as if stretched thin.

The magic of the hungry wolf shook and grumbled.

Wolf pointed at Portia Elizabeth. "Go."

She nodded and pulled on my arm. "Come," she said.

"Dire wolves," I whispered. Wolf had threatened to feed me to the magical manifestations of two animals that had gone extinct ten thousand years ago.

Wolf grinned.

Portia pulled on my arm. "Back away slowly."

Wolf smirked, but the two dire wolves backed off. Portia Elizabeth bowed her head to Wolf. It nodded once.

She pulled me toward the bar.

"I'm to hunt that old lady troll? What is Wolf going to do to her if I find her? What if I refuse?"

Portia Elizabeth shook her head as if to tell me to be quiet. She put a finger to her lips and pulled me down the steps to the bar area.

A massive, dark wood bar with an equally massive overhang ran at least twenty seats down the wall of the saloon. The entire structure—from the stool bases, to the foot rests, the counter, the back of the bar with its mirror, to the overhead storage—had been carved from one piece of wood.

The sweet, woodsy scent of spring rose from the section closest to the booths, but as we walked along the bar, the scent changed to the warm humidity of living fields, then to the crisp, brisk air of falling leaves, and finally the bitter iciness of a blizzard.

The bar was one tree—one *world*—intricately carved for the gods themselves.

The mirror behind the bar reflected... magic. Maybe the universe. But I was not looking at myself or even the Crossroads Saloon.

It was too much. Too much restaurant noise. Too much dislocation. Too much being pulled away from my own mind and my own body.

"Stop gaping," Portia Elizabeth said.

"I am not gaping," I snapped. I stopped walking instead. "Explain what just happened." I held out my arm. "This is the same magic as your dress, isn't it?"

She nodded.

The magic coiled and roiled in its spot on my forearm, just as much as the not-right perceptions my eyes and ears were picking up coiled and roiled in my head. "It's not dark magic, is it?" It didn't feel dark. Nor did it feel light, either. It felt bigger than me, and old, as if it was too old to be either dark or light. "What *is* this?"

She shook her head.

"I need to know what's happening. Why are you working for Wolf?" Especially if her dress was as powerful as I suspected it to be.

The resonance of her magic changed again. "Find the troll, Frank Victorsson," she said. "Bring her to House."

"Yes." *No,* I thought. "I see your magic changing. I feel it touching me. I know what you are doing." My head spun.

"Frank." She gripped my cheeks.

I pulled away. My foot slid back, and my hand swung to my side and brushed a barstool. A chill hit my arms. We were at the end of the bar closest to the door, where winter drifted off the wood. "Why do you allow Wolf to control you?"

Portia Elizabeth pushed me in an attempt to move me toward the doors.

Sometimes my mind splits when a rage starts. Sometimes I'm aware of the ragings as I rage. I know what I'm doing. I hear my own voice yelling that the rages are not what I want. That I am better than that. That I left the anger behind on the same ice on which I left my father to die.

But he escaped, and so did my rage.

My hands wrapped around the seat of a barstool. It shouldn't have come loose—it didn't want to come loose—but my father also baked into my semi-dead body strength it should not have.

I threw the seat over Portia Elizabeth's head. It flew through the glamours and magicks of Crossroads Saloon toward the Wolf's booth and vanished into the shadows of the universe.

"I need the dress!" Portia Elizabeth's red dress rose up around her like the shroud of death itself. "You called me a succubus. Tell me how I am to walk in the world and not be a monster, Frank Victorsson! I cannot love anyone. I cannot live. I destroy the worlds people build. I destroy lives."

Her green magic screamed upward through its resonance range—it built and built until it, like the dress, rose up like Death's shroud. "Isolation or death—those are my choices. Those are *everyone's* choices! Even yours."

"No," I said. Isolation and death were not the only choices. "If you don't want this enchantment, I can help. The elves can—"

The elves can... A memory sliced through my rage and hit me full force. A human woman. We were on the side of the road not far from my home. She had a green bike, and...

She was enchanted.

Portia Elizabeth stepped back from me as if she was afraid her magic would disrupt my memories—as if she somehow understood what my memories were.

She inhaled sharply. "Raven," she said.

Raven was there, between us, in her hipster clothes and her much-too-knowing grin. She looked me over once, then looked to Portia Elizabeth. They both frowned.

And the last thing I remember was Raven snapping her fingers against my forehead.

CHAPTER 19

Two hundred years of sleeping like the dead has left me with a utilitarian view of my dreams. Such a view seems counter-intuitive at first because each night is a dance on the edge of The Land of the Dead. A single, slow breath is a step around an open pit of spinning ghosts. A flutter of my eyelids is a waltz with jealous shades who would make me one of their own.

I sleep cold, yet I should dream in humming adrenaline.

But a life lived properly is not a life full of dread. I do not fear my sleep no matter how I wish it were something other than the stiff, isolating thing that it is. I do not gnash my teeth and wail at my father's cruelty. At least, not anymore.

So my sleep is what it is—the cold time when my body recovers its balance from the day. It may be bitter, and it may be frightening to the few women I have trusted to spend the night in my bed, but without it, my scars would not have faded. My bones would not have knitted and my muscles grown coherent. My sleep, like everyone else's, is what keeps me alive.

But now ribbons of red magic wove through my pedestrian dreams of walking hotel halls and avoiding blond fake-elves. Ribbons that snapped outward from a brand on my arm toward unsuspecting elves and wolves, only to transform into a roaring maw that ate both the sun and the moon. Red ribbons that wrapped themselves through my sleep and choked away my cold and my rest….

Someone pounded on my hotel room door.

I gasped awake as if I hadn't been breathing at all—as if a gag had been over my mouth and nose and no matter how my lungs tried, I couldn't pull in air.

I touched my throat and my chest. No ribbons of red magic. No silk from Portia Elizabeth's dress. I was alone in my dark room with my brain hammering on the walls of my skull—and someone hammering on the door.

The room was thankfully dark. My bag sat on the dresser next to the television. The curtains were pulled, which explained the precious darkness, but the sun leaking in around the edges suggested it was afternoon. And I had been crosswise on the made-up bed, in the same clothes I wore when we left for the apartments, like someone had dumped me and run.

"Frank!" Remy yelled through the door. He pounded again and the entire hotel felt as if it pounded with him. "Please tell me you're in there."

Remy. He was okay.

He slapped the door again. "Come on, Frank. Answer the door."

My head throbbed. Why did I have a hangover? My body stayed within its baseline no matter how I abused it. My quick healing was pretty much the only attribute for which I thanked my father.

I slowly stood up. "Hold on," I groaned.

"She zapped us," Remy said through the door. "She hasn't seen me for three centuries and I don't even get a 'How are you?' She just sends me away."

I staggered toward the entrance.

"I tried your phone but you didn't answer—"

I swung open the door. "Can you hear yourself?"

He threw up his hands. "What?"

The hall light buzzed as much as it glared, and I squinted. "Did you ask *her* how *she* was?" This was not an argument I wanted to get into right now. I waved him into the room, mostly so I didn't have to hear the buzzing of the fluorescents in the hallway. I was barely tracking what Remy said.

His lip twitched and he pushed into my room. He ignored my question. "Why didn't you answer your phone?"

Because I was zapped, I thought.

I patted at my pocket. No phone. It wasn't on the dresser next to the television, either. "The kitsune stole it," I mumbled.

Zapped and zapped again.

"When?" Remy's already high incredulousness set his lip twitching again. "How?" He dropped his hand to his back pocket and covered his own as he looked around me and back out into the hallway.

"They showed up when Portia Elizabeth sent you home."

He stepped back to get a better look down the hall, then he gave me a once-over. "That apartment complex messes with *time*, Frank. We're—what the hell is on your arm?"

I looked down at my forearm, then shook my head and walked toward the bed.

"Did the kitsune *burn* you?" His disbelief foamed over into a muscle-tensing anger.

"The kitsune didn't do this, Remy." I held out my arm again. No matter how much I wanted back my phone, we had bigger issues. "They didn't give me the hangover, either."

I rubbed my head. When enchantments mess with space and time, they also mess with memory, and I'd been messed with big-time last night.

I had yet another hole in my map of my life.

I pulled back my arm to swing at the wall, but Remy stopped me.

"Whoa! Hey! No more destroying hotel property. Mr. Lost My Hair has enough on us." Remy pushed me toward the bed. "He's lying about the ponytail, by the way. I bet a panda gnawed it off."

"Pandas are gentle." I unclenched my fist, my arm, and my shoulder. Remy was correct; I needed to breathe and not trip over my own potholes.

"I *know*." Remy walked over to the mini-fridge and pulled out a bottle of water. He shook his head. "I'm going to find out what *really* happened. We need dirt on him."

I walked toward the bed. We did need dirt on the usurper. But right now, I needed him to help me figure out what was happening with the non-elven magicals.

"Bears, my fluffy wolf ass," he said.

This bear-beef with Niklas der Nord was going to be an issue—not one I had any intention of smoothing over or interfering with in any way, but an issue nonetheless. Often it was best to allow the wolves to finish their stalkings, and with Remy, it was best to let him be a... wolf.

I'd come face-to-face with a major Wolf spirit last night.

"We have bigger problems than Nik of the North and his absent hair," he said.

I stared at my arm. "Obviously."

"Do you remember what happened?" Remy asked. "You stumbled off. I was sure you'd already gone out to the SUV, but you weren't there when I walked out. I couldn't get back in to look for you."

He pulled his phone from his pocket. "When I unlocked my phone to call you, I had twenty-five messages from Arne wondering where we were."

He held it out.

I peered at the screen, but rubbed my eyes when they wouldn't focus.

"It's *Thursday morning*," Remy said as he walked in to my room. "We went out there Sunday night. They stole three days from us."

"What?" All the colors of his screen swam around in much the same way as natural magic. "That's not possible."

"Oh, yes it is." Remy paced between the dresser and the bed. "It takes skill, but a well-placed stasis spell can steal time." Remy threw his hands into the air. "I called Arne on the drive back here. They were already on their plane. They should be landing shortly." He slapped the wall. "Thank Odin's eyeball you were here."

Someone kidnapped me, stole three days, and... made me an offer I couldn't refuse.

I held up my arm. "Remy, Portia Elizabeth did this to me on the orders of a Wolf spirit."

Remy stopped with the bottle halfway to his mouth, then he exhaled and took a sip. "What? Not *my* wolf spirit."

"Of course not yours," I said. "It claimed to be, but it seemed too specifically Las Vegas to be the werewolf spirit."

He frowned.

"That's not the main issue here. I chased the kitsune and ended up getting kidnapped by Raven. She and Portia Elizabeth took me into the desert. Turns out Raven traded my offer of service to this Wolf spirit, who is some sort of local crime boss." I laid on the soft comfort of the big bed.

"What'd she get for you?" The speed of Remy's pacing increased.

"I have no idea. Probably some extra-shiny doodad." Why hadn't the hangover cleared yet? I was having difficulty piecing together what had happened.

I sniffed at my t-shirt. Probably because of the… troll scat.

The troll. I was supposed to find her. I *had* to find her *now* or I became dire wolf puppy chow.

"This was supposed to be simple," I said. "We fly in. We find Portia Elizabeth. We buy her dinner, you two talk about old times, and she does Arne a favor."

It was supposed to be Portia Elizabeth in red corporate attire standing in front of the Conclave Feast table with a laser pointer as she ran through slides detailing the positive impact of negative magicals on a local economy. Donuts, coffee, and a dose of cutthroat magical politics for everyone.

Then we go home. No old-school Las Vegas mob threats. No tricksters, Japanese or otherwise. No strange red magical branding. And most certainly no harassing of little old ladies, trollness notwithstanding.

I rubbed my forehead and pulled the scatted shirt over my head. I tossed it into the corner.

Remy tapped his water bottle against the dresser. "Where did they take you?"

"A Great Hall. Someplace called the Crossroads Saloon." I stood and walked toward the window.

He stared at me expectantly.

"I need to find the troll by this evening. The one who scatted us. If I don't, the Las Vegas Wolf spirit is going to feed me to its dire wolf pups."

"That sounds violent," Remy said.

I held out my new shirt and the brand. "I can't leave Las Vegas. I can't remove the mark."

Remy took another sip of his water. "We don't have time for your trickster problems, Frank," Remy said. "The Conclave Feast is tonight. Arne needs you here."

The hangover began to clear, and my headache lessened, but a shower would help. "I know."

"You're not going to find the troll in the daylight, anyway." Remy pointed at the window.

I still had to look. Maybe I should try to get the brand off, no matter the threats. I picked at the edges of the brand.

Fire surged through my skin to my bones. My entire arm felt as if it waged a battle on itself. "I stopped!" I said to the brand.

I swear it *humphed*. Was it talking to me the same way Sal talked?

"Go away," I said to the brand. I had a history of being able to hear magical items. Portia Elizabeth's dress talked to her, and this was the same magic, so perhaps the brand would talk to me. "I don't want you."

I understood the growl, but didn't hear it. The brand growled in much the same way that Sal tossed me comprehension.

"So that's how it's going to be, huh?" I said to my arm. "What if I refuse to harass the troll?"

Fire screamed up my arm again.

"Okay, okay, okay," I muttered.

"Is it talking to you?" Remy moved closer.

"It's part of Portia Elizabeth's dress," I said. "It talks to her, so this little smudge should talk to me."

The brand growled again.

"You're a bit one-note," I said to the magic.

Remy stiffened. "She gave you part of her dress?" He dropped the water bottle onto the dresser.

"She didn't *give* me anything," I said. "Wolf made her inflict it on me."

Remy poked at the brand.

A jolt of hot pain ran up my arm. "Hey!" I yanked away. "Not helping."

Remy's magic shifted into the sheets of moonglow that appeared before his wolf surfaced. "Why didn't she take me?" He poked at the brand again.

"Because I was stupid enough to offer my services," I said. "And I'm big enough to bring in the troll." Though I had my doubts about that.

Remy sniffed at the brand. His magic flared. "Portia Elizabeth is *my* mate, not yours."

Not good, I thought. I did not need an under-the-influence were-wolf mad at me on top of my troll predicament.

I pulled away my arm. "First, this has nothing to do with your wolf hormones," I said. "Second, I think you're still feeling the effects of her influence from last night—Sunday night."

He stiffened again.

His phone pinged. He turned away, pulled it out, and looked at the message. "They've landed."

"Give me that." I wiggled my fingers.

Remy frowned, but handed over his phone.

Frank here, I tapped to Arne. *Don't go to your hotel. We need you ASAP.*

Understand, appeared. *We will be there in twenty minutes.*

"They're coming directly here." I handed back his phone. "Can you keep it together until then?"

"This from the man who feels a burning need to chase down a troll."

Remy said "troll" and the brand sniffed at the magic of the hotel like a puppy scenting bacon treats.

My ability to see magic erupted into a level of perception way beyond the visual. Mr. Left and Mr. Right were, at that very moment, standing outside the Feast banquet room debating whether one of them should get coffee. Niklas der Nord worked with a set of security sigils at the back of the room. The Alfheim elves were not within the magic's range, but another set of elves approached the hotel.

A touched family, three floors down, fussed with their Con costumes. A low-powered magical dealt out cards in the casino.

And the cantankerous little old lady troll, who was only here because the desert helped her arthritis, played slots no more than fifty feet from where Remy and I ate dinner Sunday night.

The extra sensing shut off as fast as it manifested. "Whoa," I said.

"What?" Remy sniffed at the brand again.

The troll was in the casino. She played slots, but she had her suitcase at her feet. "I need to take care of this." I pushed by Remy and jogged for the elevators.

CHAPTER 20

R emy twisted through the closing elevator doors just as I hit the
button for the lobby. "Where are we going?" he asked as he
smoothed the front of his shirt.

The elevator robotically chatted out the floor levels as we
descended. "Down," I said.

He sniffed the air. "Is that troll in the building?" He sniffed again.
"Why would she be here?"

"Maybe she's here to annoy you," I said. "You did chase her into the
sunlight."

Remy *humphed*.

"Maybe she sensed the elves and wants to piss them off. She *is* a
troll." I shrugged. "Either way, ElfCon provides cover for any new
glamour breakage." She had her bag with her. "I suspect she's about to
leave for the airport."

I'd walk into the casino and...

I didn't know how the "and" would play out. Would the red magic
jump from me to her? Would she go full troll and destroy the slots?
Would she stay in glamour, scream, flail, and tell security that the
huge man threatened to hurt her little old lady self? Would Portia
Elizabeth walk in and take her away? How was I supposed to get her

to the House apartments if she didn't want to go? She was bigger than me.

"For all we know, Raven sent her and this is a setup." Remy paced as the elevator dinged through its last floors. "You, my friend, are likely walking into a trickster trap."

He was probably correct. The troll was the bait to which I could not say no, and the brand on my arm was a spring-loaded, neck-breaking mechanism.

I held out my arm again. "Get *off* me," I growled. Never again would I be kind or courteous to a trickster.

The red magic snarled, and flared. Once again, I had an intimate understanding of the locations of every single magical and magic-touched person within the hotel. I knew the directions they moved, if they chewed on a granola bar, or if they needed a nap.

I leaned against the elevator wall. "Do you growl and snap at Portia Elizabeth?" I asked my arms. "No wonder she wanted us to leave her alone."

Now the brand *humphed*.

The elevator door slid open.

Remy's phone chirped. "Arne wants you to go back to your room."

The entire concourse was jammed with Con-goers. A pair of teenagers in bright, cartoonish costumes ran by. A large man with a full beard, a wide leather belt, blue stripes on his face, and a fake wolf skin draped over his head and shoulders flexed as he walked by the elevators. Someone burped. Laughter and groans followed.

I pushed my way out of the elevator and through a gaggle of skinny fake-elves. ElfCon's major events started today, and every hotel patron other than Remy and me was in full regalia, all looking to out-elf and -character each other. Someone yelled something about winning the costume contest.

A large man in a bear costume walked by.

"Wonder what der Nord thinks of that," Remy said.

"Focus," I responded.

I waded into the crowd, with Remy following. A skinny guy in a red and black spandex suit jogged toward me and I pulled up so as not to run him over.

He pushed his fists into his hips and cocked his head. "You're big!" He pointed at my chest. "Who are you cosplaying, dude?" he asked.

"I'm not here for the convention." I stepped to the side to move around him.

He held his ground. "Oh! *So* manly!" Mr. Red and Black danced around and blew me a kiss. "You must be a frost giant!"

"Get out of my way," I said.

Remy crossed his arms, stepped to the side, and grinned. Mr. Red and Black clapped, then posed as if shooting an arrow at the moon. "Onward to Valhalla!" Then he giggled again and ran toward a group of fake-elves.

He wasn't the only normal in some variation of the red and black costume. The Con had an infestation.

"Tell the next one you're a professional wrestler." Remy pointed over his shoulder at the elevators. "Are you going to listen to Arne?"

I *should* listen. "Troll." I pointed at the other end of the concourse, the lobby, and the entrance to the casino.

Remy's wolf magic brightened. "Let's see if the magic will jump to me." He held out his arm. "I'll take it." He danced in front of me. "I'm a wolf."

A wolf who thought three hundred years wasn't enough time to kill his affair with a woman everyone thought of as a succubus.

I stopped walking in the middle of the concourse floor, about fifteen feet beyond the elevator lobby, and within full view of the Feast banquet room doors.

Magic flared up and over the heads of the Con-goers. Bright, blinding magic as each and every one of the elves threw up their own gearwork, sheets, sigils, and walls.

Elven magic.

"Remy…"

"I bet half the mundanes here felt that," Remy said.

"I hope not." The last thing we needed was a touched mundane having a heart attack because they felt "a ghost."

The door to the Feast banquet room opened. More magic poured out, as did a lovely, real, golden light.

The Siberian twins exited first. Mr. Left moved unsurprisingly to the left, and Mr. Right to the right. The twins had glamoured themselves back to their *Matrix* dark suits, white shirts, sunglasses, and earpieces.

Niklas der Nord exited next. He continued to semi-glamour enough to appear as a mundane in a costume, and still wore his wine-red leathers.

A new, tightly-packed group of real elves walked toward the Feast room. A bubble of magic kept all the mundane Con-goers at least ten feet away on all sides.

One of the Courts approached the Conclave Feast.

Der Nord quickly made his way from the room entrance toward the approaching elves.

The male in the center of the bubble was visibly smaller than the other elves, and about five inches shorter than der Nord. Two other elves, both female and just as uptight and cinched-up as the male in the center, stood with their hands behind their backs as if they were the small elf's very own Siberian twins. The two female elves were in full glamour with no overt elf-ness showing. Both were smartly—and comfortably—dressed, even if they did appear particularly uncomfortable.

They weren't guards. They were this Court's Queen and Elder.

The elf in the middle, like the women, was in full, unassuming glamour with unkempt clothes, a bit of a belly, and a receding hairline.

"Bragisson," Remy said. He quickly pulled out his phone.

Gearwork magic very much like Dag's slid and locked around the Elf Emperor. His was darker in color, and somehow more complex, even if it didn't at first glance show how, or why.

The cloud of elf magic filling the lobby was drenched in his signature, leaving no doubt about who was in charge.

The Elf Emperor himself, wearing just as much of a costume as the ElfCon's attendees, chatted with Niklas der Nord out in the open, in the center of the concourse, as his daughter and her disappointing husband were pulling up outside.

"Do we hide?" Remy asked.

They were standing between me and the casino. Hiding was not an option.

Magic flared upward from Bragisson and he stepped to the side of der Nord. He looked around, then threw his arms wide.

"Mr. Geroux!" he called.

"Too late," Remy said. He quickly texted something to Arne, then tucked away his phone as we walked over.

Bragisson stood eye-to-eye with Remy and greeted him with a shoulder slap. He extended his hand to me. "You must be Frank Victorsson! It's a pleasure," he said in perfect, impeccable English. "Allow me to introduce our Empress, Astrid Heimdallsdottir, and our Second, Þórdís Ullrsdottir."

I bowed my head. "Welcome to Las Vegas."

Bragisson laughed and slapped his thigh. "Now *you* have manners, unlike those vampires, huh?" He winked.

The Emperor of the Elves made a bad, gossipy joke and winked like everyone's bad boss everywhere.

The affable elf business had to be a front. Nothing I'd ever heard about Tyr Bragisson led me to believe the elf in front of me was *nice*. Not his political dealings. Not the constant yelling over the phone that made Akeyla unhappy. Not Dag's near-omnipresent frowns concerning all things Bragisson. Not Arne's silence.

But mostly the fact that this elf had not once stepped foot in Alfheim since he married off his daughter to the New World king.

Remy looked as suspicious as I felt. Der Nord stepped back. Bragisson's Queen and Elder ignored the conversation.

Bragisson clasped his hands behind his back. "My son-in-law sent ahead his attendants." He frowned like an uptight librarian.

"As did you." Remy grinned the sweetest, friendliest grin I'd ever seen him flash at an elf. "We're all here to check out the facilities, no?"

Bragisson frown deepened. Then he, too, grinned sweetly. "Yes, yes. For security," he said.

Remy bowed as if offering our services, as well.

His phone chirped. I glanced at the other end of the concourse before realizing what I was doing. What if Arne or Dag arrived and cut me off before I reached the casino?

I yanked on Remy's arm. "Excuse us, King Bragisson, Queen Heimdallsdottir, Elder Ullrsdottir," I said. "Remy and I would like to keep as close to protocol as possible."

"Niklas tells me you had a run-in with a troll." Bragisson's tone was not sweet, nor was it friendly. His glamour kept its ignorable balding-middle-aged-man look and feel, and his magic continued to be a shifting, layered, indigo-violet version of Dag's gearwork, but my instincts stood up and took notice.

"Trolls are a problem," he said. "The entire lot of them."

Bragisson had no idea she was in the building. None of the elves appeared to know.

The brand on my arm snickered.

I resisted glancing at it. The less Bragisson knew about my predicament, the better. At least until I could have Arne or Dag look it over.

He probably also knew every detail of our earlier troll encounter, and the resulting fallout. Niklas der Nord could have simply been reporting information to Bragisson, or he could have been strategically destroying our credibility.

My money was on destruction. *Snitch*, I thought. At least he hadn't realized yet that she was nearby.

A small, almost imperceptible sneer flickered along der Nord's upper lip.

Remy leaned closer to Bragisson. "She said she was on vacation. Seems the desert eases troll arthritis. Not their cranky attitudes, unfortunately." He shrugged. "I would love to tell you the entire story after the Feast, sir." He grinned again. "It's an entertaining tale."

Bragisson chuckled. "Our trolls enjoy harassing mundane road-building crews." He shook his head. "We have two who will occasionally toss boulders into our enclave. The Danish enclave has had a handful of problems lately. Seems the trolls claim one of their elves is a thief."

"Fascinating," I said. "Excuse us."

Der Nord stepped between us and the lobby end of the concourse.

Did he know something? He had to.

Remy's phone chirped again.

Der Nord's eyes narrowed as he watched a laughing clutch of Con-goers walk by. They didn't have elven politics to worry about, or World Spirits threatening their homes and families. They were here to have fun, and to enjoy Las Vegas's wonders.

Remy's werewolf magic fluttered. It shifted into a wolf form, and the curtains of energy thickened and condensed, as his aurora yellows and greens changed to blues and purples.

Der Nord's actions irritated Remy. He'd been itchy around der Nord during every interaction we'd had. And now his laser-focus had once again come around to the one elf who could cause the Alfheim elves the most trouble.

Remy moved toward Bragisson. "I have never been to your island or met one of your trolls." He looked around as if sharing a secret, then leaned closer to Bragisson. "You do know our work? My brother and I?"

Der Nord moved to pull Remy away from Bragisson.

Remy threw his arms up and stepped back in a way only the werewolves moved—he unconsciously dropped the center of his weight and poised his legs for a lunging bounce.

Der Nord stepped in front of Bragisson as if to take the hit in case Remy went feral. Bragisson shook his head, and his body language shifted into the smug righteousness of a politician who took the power of his political position for granted.

A new, bright flash of magic burst from the main lobby end of the concourse, and a light blue-green sigil formed in the air above the Con-goers.

The three Icelandic elves looked over their shoulders.

Dagrun Tyrsdottir moved like an arrow through the crowd toward her father, ex-husband, and us. She wore a glamour as boringly middle American as her father's, but she wanted the other elves to know she could still out-enchant them, even with a cast on her arm.

Her magic lifted upward and over our heads as if purposefully flooding the concourse with precision spellwork.

"Father," Dagrun said as she walked up. "Astrid. Þórdís." Nothing else. No comments about itineraries or notifications. Just a single icy acknowledgement of the Icelandic Court.

Bragisson's magic solidified, and for a split second, I wondered if he would attack his own daughter. He beckoned her forward and extended his arms instead.

She offered no physical touch. No hug or kiss to the cheek. She clasped her hands behind her back instead, in much the same way her father had earlier. Next to me, Remy sniffed as if holding in a snicker.

"Why the theatrics?" Dag asked. She wasn't looking at her father. She watched der Nord.

"As hosts, we are here ahead of the delegations." Bragisson waved his hand at Remy and me. "Where is your husband, daughter? We must establish the room for official greetings. The Conclave begins shortly."

"Arne will arrive momentarily." Dag lowered the pitch of her voice. "I wish to speak to our pack and our paladin."

Not once had I heard any of the elves officially declare me *paladin*. I'd always been their jotunn and their adopted son, but never their warrior. But the way Dag said "pack and paladin" made it clear, at least to me, that they considered Alfheim's non-elven residents as important to the enclave as the elves.

My surprise surprised me. I lived in Alfheim. I had for the majority of my two hundred years. Whenever I left, I always came home to a family who welcomed me with open arms. They even took in my own adopted witch daughter, but "paladin" was just as much of a joke as "jotunn" and "Biterson."

To hear the clear intent in Dag's voice as she spoke to other elves caught me off guard.

Remy, though, grinned like the wolf he was.

Niklas der Nord extended his hand to Dag. His expression took on a loose, wide-eyed longing that his body did not mirror. "Dagrun," he said in a reverent, sweet voice.

He took her casted hand, and kissed the plaster.

"Niklas." The ice that had coated Dagrun's voice when she spoke to her father cracked when she spoke to der Nord. Some warmth made it through.

She peered at his unglamoured hair and lack-of-ponytail.

Remy sniffed and twirled his finger behind his head. "Arne never had an issue with bears," he said.

Dagrun neither twitched, sneered, nor laughed. "There *was* that one grizzly in Yellowstone." A hint of sarcasm made it into the ice in her voice, though. "Amazing creatures. Much meaner than your average Eurasian brown bear."

"Arne's never lost *anything* at *all* to a bear," Remy said.

This wasn't his wolf working through Remy. This was his hooligan dancing out in front of his pack as a distraction to a major predator. Every one of his pokes at der Nord was to distract him from harming the Alfheim Pack's elven members. I knew it. Dag knew it. But right now, we didn't need our high-strung Alpha picking a fight with a powerful elf.

Too late. Der Nord turned on Remy. His glamour flickered.

"Excuse us!" I half-yelled. Anything to distract the elf and the werewolf. "We have business." I pointed over their heads toward the casino.

All the elves looked at me.

"Remy and I will report to the entire Conclave at the beginning of the Feast," I said.

"You and your wolf will explain *now*." Der Nord continued to stare at Remy. "No more instigating behaviors we must cover," he said. "For the mundanes' protection."

He was baiting Remy.

Dagrun cleared her throat. "Frank and Remy will report to *all* the Courts as is Conclave protocol." Her lips and the muscles around her eyes tightened, as did her magic. It shifted outward and sliced between Remy and her father, between der Nord and me, but mostly between der Nord and herself.

"The Feast, then, Father?" she said.

No need to fight in public, her magic said.

The threat of a private fight was not lost on Bragisson. "The Feast, yes. Your Mr. Victorsson will report then, daughter." He motioned to the two female guards. "Olav and Bjorn have landed and are preparing themselves now."

Olav Sigundsson, the Siberian King, and Bjorn Bjornsson, the Norwegian. They would both likely arrive shortly with underlings from their subordinate enclaves.

Bragisson looked between us and Dag. "You stay." Nothing else. No pleasantries or requests, only a command issued to his daughter.

Remy opened his mouth, but Dag held up her hand. "Go on," she said.

Der Nord backed away from Remy. He bowed to Dagrun and lifted her hand to his lips once again. "Come," he said. He turned to follow Bragisson toward the conference rooms and—

Lollipop appeared just off der Nord's shoulder. She'd pulled her hair into a ponytail mimicking the elves' and had morphed her clothes into an exact duplicate of der Nord's wine-red leathers.

Remy bared his teeth.

Every elf around us responded as if attacked. Every one of them lifted their hands to toss out some sort of magical protection.

Except they weren't looking at the kitsune. They were all looking at Remy.

Lollipop winked. She pulled a Santa-shaped candy from her mouth and tapped it against Niklas's cheek.

She vanished.

"Kitsune!" I grabbed Remy's arm just as he raised it to swipe at Lollipop.

He would have hit der Nord with a well-placed right hook.

Dag tossed out a magical net. Þórdís Ullrsdottir stepped between Remy and me and the other elves.

By the banquet room's door, Mr. Right of the Siberian twins

glanced around the lobby as if he, too, had felt the kitsune's presence. He nodded to his brother, and a spell formed around them.

A spell that looked anti-fox.

How, I couldn't tell, because the sigil markings and the lines of energy looked like every other enchantment I'd ever seen an elf produce, except this one gave off a clear no-foxes-allowed vibe.

"Kitsune? Here? Your attendants attracted *tricksters* to the Conclave?" der Nord yelled.

Three mundane Con-goers stared. A long string of Icelandic poured from Dagrun. Her father shot back an equally stinging string. Magic flitted off both of them, and the Con-goers blinked as if waking up, but continued on their way anyway.

Bragisson turned his back to his daughter and walked toward the banquet room. His Queen and Elder followed, though neither appeared happy.

"We attracted no one," Remy growled. "They were here when we arrived."

Der Nord looked between Dag, Remy, and his boss. "They were here when you arrived and you did not inform me?"

"They're interested in me," I said. "Not you."

"And yet you expect us to allow you into the Feast banquet? You are trickster-touched." Der Nord followed Bragisson. "I told you they were not to be trusted," he yelled to his boss.

"Father!" Dagrun snapped.

Bragisson stopped walking. He lifted his chin and narrowed his eyes. "I cannot allow trickster-bringers into the Feast. You know that, daughter."

Then he walked between the Siberian twins and into the banquet room.

We just lost our chance to stand for Alfheim—and now Arne and Dag were also trickster-contaminated by association.

I'd throttle Chip and Lollipop. They were worse than brats. They were destroyers.

Dag yelled something Russian-sounding at the twins. They looked at each other, then turned in unison and also followed her father into the room.

"Remy!" I pulled him aside—which took more effort than it should have. He felt stronger, more agile. His eyes had begun to change. His wolf was surfacing now, during the day, in the lobby of a busy hotel.

"Calm down," I said. "We just lost our chance to speak at the Feast."

Dag pinched her forehead.

"One of the kitsune appeared right next to der Nord," I said. "The one with the lollipop."

She shook her head. "I did not sense or see her."

"*None* of you did," I said. "Purposefully."

Remy pushed me off. "Maybe this is why Portia Elizabeth didn't choose me. Why else would those two brats show up right now? Only to destroy."

"Remy…" I didn't know what to say.

Remy paced but did not walk away. "I'm done."

I leaned close to Dagrun. "We found Portia Elizabeth. She works for the Wolf spirit who runs the Las Vegas magicals." I glanced at Remy. "It… gave me a job."

Her magic shook. "Explain."

I held out my arm. "I made the mistake of offering my services to a trickster. Not Wolf. Raven. Now I'm a troll hunter."

Dagrun Tyrsdottir showed no physical sign of anxiety. Her expression did not change, nor did her posture. She waved her hand over the brand. "It pooled in a space left open by your stolen tracers."

I nodded.

She extended her hand toward Remy. "What of these kitsune?"

Remy twirled around. "I wonder if Arne realized that when he brought Gerard and me into Alfheim that a version of the spirit that created *my* kind might someday decide to interfere in elven business?"

"We still have you and Frank." Dag did not seem worried about the lack of Portia Elizabeth. "No matter what Niklas says."

Remy backed away. He shook his head and jogged toward the elevators.

I looked to Dag. She shook her head and waved me to follow.

"I can't," I said. "The troll is in the building. She's playing slots right now." I waved toward the other end of the concourse. "You don't sense her?"

Dag stepped closer. "Trolls figured out a long time ago how to operate in the same area as elves. If she's not actively using her magic, none of us would sense her." She looked down at my arm. "You don't need to chase her down." A wave of magic moved over me.

Nothing changed. The brand did not lift away.

Dagrun gripped my arm. Another wave of magic flowed over me, and again, nothing changed.

"I have never in my life come across magic like this," she said. "It's... visceral."

The Con-goers continued to move around us as if we were just two more mundanes. "I need to go," I said.

She gripped my cheeks. "You are no spirit's hound, Frank."

I would have hugged the elf I considered mother, but we were in public and in full view of the Siberian guards. "I know," I said. "I know."

Remy and me, we were the two guys who accidentally found ourselves in the sights of a World Spirit crime boss because we wanted to talk to the wrong person. And now I had to complete a dumb task for magicals who were not my people.

I just wanted to go home and sleep off the entire misadventure. I wanted to wake up with a clean arm again.

Remy vanished into the elevator lobby. I should have followed, but if there was one thing of which I was sure, it was that neither of us wanted to let down Portia Elizabeth.

Dag stepped back. She had her orders. I had mine.

The Elf Queen of Alfheim walked toward the Conclave banquet room, and I pushed my way through the crowd toward the casino floor.

CHAPTER 21

Lights flashed. Machines jingled. Casino-goers laughed and yelled. And the brand on my arm pressed magical information into my senses: A spirit worked the floor. The troll played slots. And two elves prowled between the games as I lumbered my way through the crowd.

A server holding a tray looked me over as I passed by. I followed the red magic's directions, and made my way into one of the more isolated rows of slots in the casino. The shadows thickened toward the machines, mostly to heighten their hypnotic effect on mundanes. For a troll, they only helped the cave-like atmosphere.

I folded myself into the reclining cushiness of the seat next to the troll's chosen slot machine. She'd picked the slots in a farthest corner, behind a blackjack table and next to one of the casino's flush-with-the-wall security doors.

The troll, still in her granite-haired, polyester-dressed, gray and lavender glamour, poked at the machine's buttons. She swiped and played, this time without a bucket of coins.

Her bag sat on the floor next to her feet. She stopped with her hand frozen mid-air, sniffed once, and pinched her entire face as if she'd just sucked on a lemon.

"Not-a-jotunn, I told you all I know." She flicked her pinky at me. "You found House. I know." She sniffed again and her face pulled into the same lemon-sucked pinch as when I first sat down. "Go away."

"I'd love to," I said.

The troll chortled. "Did *they* get you, big boy?"

Looks as if the troll knew more than she'd let on when we first found her. "Who is this *they* of whom you speak, troll?"

She pointed at my forearm. "Let me see."

I held out my arm. She sniffed at the brand, shook her head, and pushed more buttons on the jingling, whirring machine. "You poor thing," she said. "I owe that mangy yipper nothing."

I settled into the chair. Casino furniture really was comfortable. "It doesn't think so."

She shrugged. "I am old. I like a rest from the winter cold." She held up her hand and wiggled her fingers to reiterate her assertion about arthritis. "But I am one of the few of my kind willing to leave our bridges and rocks."

"I figured you were special."

"We do not glamour well." She winked. "One of its hounds helped me." She waved her hand and her glamour fluctuated.

The underlying magic wasn't Portia Elizabeth's green, or even anything that hinted at a vampire, so whoever helped the troll wasn't a magical of whom I was aware.

The troll leaned toward me. "He talked a lot about Big Fae and Big Elf, and how us less-desirable magicals needed to stick together."

I chuckled, which turned into a laugh. "The gatekeeper?"

She shrugged. "I learned. I make my own glamour." She waved her hand at her glittery jewelry and her lavender polyester blouse. "I not copy *anyone*. The mangy yipper wants *me* to pay *it* a toll because it says it owns this look in this territory."

Wolf had me hunting the troll over a frivolous copyright claim? How absurd. "The kitsune didn't set this up, did they?"

She looked over her shoulder. "Foxes? Where?"

"They're not here."

"Oh." She returned to swiping her card, yanking on levers, and pushing buttons. "I leave soon. Going home." She pointed at her bag. "Mangy yipper can eat its own tail."

"How many hounds has Wolf sent to annoy you?"

The troll tapped the slots as if counting. "You are number five."

Five?

She poked a finger in my direction. "You can go away, too, not-a-jotunn."

I leaned back in my seat. "Wolf threatened to rip me apart and feed my parts to its dire wolves if I didn't bring you back to House."

The troll laughed. "It thinks you can move *me*?" She laughed again.

This time, I was the one who shrugged.

"My plane leaves this evening. I play now. Take gold home." She nodded as if quite pleased with herself.

She swiped at the slots again. "Where's the doggie?" She glanced around me. "Lots of *elves* around." She spit out *elves* as if the word was venomous. "They partying? Maybe I demand tribute at an exit." She leaned closer. "Help to pay bills." She pointed at the machine. "Elves can afford it."

"Remy's not here," I said. "And yes, the elves are partying."

The machine whizzed and beeped, and the screen pulled up two cherries and a lemon.

The troll sighed and poked at the machine again. "You like that vampire who came looking a few days ago?" She pointed at my arm. "Vampires worse than elves." She spit out *elves* again.

The kids at House had said something about a vampire named Anthea.

The troll poked a crooked finger at my nose. "That vampire vanished into a gate." She nodded knowingly. "Strong magic, it was."

"I heard about that," I said.

The troll leaned closer again. "She was going to bind me with her magic," she pointed at the brand, "but the call from the gate was too strong."

So the troll had been saved by Dracula's timing.

"Maybe I go to Monte Carlo, next year, huh? Or Macau." She frowned. "I like the slots."

"How did you get away from the vampire?" Maybe the troll was smarter than we thought.

"I am here, aren't I?" She peered at my face. "Not too bright, are you?"

So the running out into the sunshine was more for show than an actual problem for this troll.

I leaned back in the soft, comfortable chair. "How are we supposed to deal with this?" I asked, not at all expecting the troll to answer, or to at least answer in a way that would help me. She could walk out, get on her plane, and go home. I couldn't force her to do anything she didn't want to do, not that I was inclined to do so, anyway.

The troll coughed out a laugh. "Buy me whiskey, not-a-jotunn."

I was surprised she hadn't yet asked me for gold. "What's your name?" I asked. "Since I'm buying you whiskey."

The troll's next poke was directed at my eye. "Oh, no, you not get my *name*, big boy." She sniffed again. "Don't trust. You live with elves and old wolves." She shook her head as if I'd committed the biggest sin in the entire universe.

I shrugged. "Fair enough."

I stood and looked around, half expecting to see Portia Elizabeth striding through the casino toward the troll.

Carrying around this need to not disappoint a female fertility spirit—not a desire, or even an impulse, just a need—had added a thick new layer to my fatigue. Or perhaps the absurdity of the past few days had fully caught up with me.

The troll cackled. "Whiskey!"

On the other side of the casino, across the lobby and down the ElfCon concourse, the elves "partied," and the Alfheim Court was about to make a case for the continued building of bridges in a world where those bridges sometimes let in vampires.

And here I stood, branded by a crime boss with magic I neither wanted nor understood, waiting out the proceedings with an attitudinal troll.

Perhaps I should buy us both whiskeys.

I stepped out of the shadows and away from the slots. The overheads brightened in the walking area, and the carpet reflected the light in much the same way as moss clinging to a troll's rocks.

I looked around again, hoping to see the server.

Magnus Freyrsson walked along the main corridor through the casino, his glamour exquisitely high-roller even though his hands were creating traveling concealment enchantments specifically for the mundanes around him and his companion.

Arne Odinsson walked at his side, and Arne Odinsson was not alone.

The impression that formed in my mind, the distinct and purposeful transfer of information, was meant for the brand on my arm as much as it was for me.

He's mine! Sal yelled in the magical way only an elven battle axe could yell.

CHAPTER 22

Arne brought my axe into the casino, and my axe was not happy about the invasive magic on my forearm.

Not happy at all. Sal glowed. Every single sigil marking, rune, and engraving on her blade screamed in magical elven light. If it weren't for Magnus's spells, the entire casino floor would have been lit up like a movie set.

The troll screamed. "Troll killer!" She threw her swipe card and an old drink at me.

"They're not here for you!" I yelled.

Her glamour flickered. She rose up, towering over me, and swung her arms as if wild swings would be enough to keep the elves and Sal away.

Arne flipped Sal to his other shoulder and held up his hand. Like Magnus, he was dressed impeccably in an expensive, well-tailored suit that included all the jewelry one would expect of a high roller—gold cufflinks and chains, a big ruby ring, and a Rolex. His elven ponytail swung behind his head, though, and his ears only carried enough glamour to look fake enough that the mundanes would think he was here for ElfCon.

"Troll!" Arne shouted. "Two ingots of gold and a bag of silver bullion for your cooperation!"

The troll stopped in mid-swing. "Bullion?" Her glamour stabilized. "For cooperation?"

Arne and Magnus stopped about ten feet away. Arne motioned to me. "Sal went crazy Sunday night. Maura said she started glowing and yelling. That's how we knew you and Remy had been caught in a distortion enchantment."

He dropped Sal into his hands. "The ragings began this morning when she picked up your scent again, saying that you'd been 'contaminated' and demanding that we bring her along."

Sal threw detailed threats of violence at the brand on my arm. Magical violence that felt strangely similar to the dislike she'd shown toward the Odin's Gallows dagger.

"I can't carry her right now," I said. "Incompatible magic." I held up my arm.

Magnus scoffed. "What did Portia Elizabeth do to you?"

Arne peered at the brand. "Promise me you will never again offer services to a trickster."

"You offered services to a trickster?" the troll said. "Is that how you got in this mess? You stupid."

Magnus held out his hands the way he would when approaching an angry dog, and slowly walked toward the troll. "Madame," he said. "We wish to make a deal." He escorted her deeper into the shadows for a chat.

Arne nodded toward the brand. "I'm sorry I sent you and Remy into this alone. I should have sent Magnus with you. None of this would have happened if you'd had an elf at your back."

I watched the troll do a little happy bounce. "Magnus would have been a blatant breaking of Conclave protocol." As was bringing Sal.

"I don't care." Arne stared in the direction of the troll, too. "*My* elves would not have allowed outside interference with the Conclave proceedings."

And there it was, the Elf King of Alfheim's arrogance. But it wasn't really arrogance when he was correct.

"How is this supposed to play out? Will Portia Elizabeth come down to collect the troll?" Arne's magic brightened and strengthened into a wall around not only him, but me as well.

"I'm supposed to take her to the apartment complex Mark Ellis talked about. I don't know what will happen if I don't."

He nodded. "Portia Elizabeth is in the building."

The brand flicked out an awareness of the magicals again. Portia Elizabeth knocked on Remy's door.

She'd been near since I woke up, but just outside the brand's range. She'd been watching, and even though she had been forbidden from helping, she hadn't been forbidden from visiting her mate.

So visit, she did.

The extra perceiving clicked off. Sal shrieked at the brand, which shrieked back at her.

"I *have* to get this thing off me."

Arne peered at it again. "Looks that way."

"Did you know that Las Vegas has a Wolf spirit who has claimed the city as its territory? It leashed Portia Elizabeth, too. Neither of us has a lot of control here."

Just like Dag, Arne waved his hands over the brand. And also just like with Dag, nothing changed.

"The entire world is some Wolf or another's territory," he said. "Raven's too." He hit the brands with a spike of magic.

The red magic growled at Arne. Pain ratcheted up my arm and into my shoulder.

"I am not familiar with this magic. It's not reacting like any spell or enchantment I've ever encountered."

"I think it's new magic. Wolf said 'adapt or die.'" Or perhaps it was repurposed old magic. Whatever it was, it held tight to my skin.

Arne tapped the brand. "Call your mistress," he said.

The brand growled at him again—and zapped me with the omniscient, overwhelming understanding of the magicals in the hotel.

"The Siberian Court has arrived." I shielded my eyes as if cutting the glare would stop the red magic's harassment. "The Norwegian Court comes with elders from all their subordinate enclaves." The building was filling with elves—fake and real—and all the noise that came with them.

"Enough of that," Arne said, and wrapped a tight band of blue elven magic around my forearm.

The brand fell silent. It seethed still, but Arne's spell acted as a gag. At least it would no longer randomly flare my ability to see magic.

Sal calmed a bit, but continued to do her version of glaring at the invader on my arm.

Arne looked toward the lobby and concourse beyond it. Dagrun was the only member of the Alfheim Court in the Feast banquet room. Not Arne, who was the reason for the Conclave in the first place. Not Magnus, either. "Dagrun needs us," he said.

"I can't enter the Feast," I said. "Niklas der Nord kicked Remy and me out because we're trickster-touched."

Arne scowled. "I will bloody that pathetic fool."

"We are agreed!" Magus called.

Arne grinned as he shouldered Sal again. "Come, son, let us face the Conclave of Elves."

CHAPTER 23

The troll's name was Ragnar, and she liked the idea of investigating the multitude of Minnesota's tribal gaming opportunities, even if it meant cold temperatures in the winter. The issues with Wolf had turned her off to Las Vegas, but not America.

Magnus offered up access to his charter air company, plus free glamouring lessons for any of her troll family who also wished to visit, along with the two ingots of gold and a bag full of silver.

Looked as if the casinos of Minnesota were about to become the prime vacation destination for Danish trolls.

As per Conclave protocol, Ragnar released her glamour when we reached the lobby end of the concourse. She looked out over ElfCon's participants, nodded once to Arne, and revealed her true, nine-foot, rocky self.

The mundanes gasped. Applause broke out, and Ragnar bowed graciously.

Magnus walked ahead of her, tossing out cards for a physical effects company in which he also owned partial interest. Seemed he hadn't fully left behind his Hollywood days, and had been funding a small production house since the thirties.

Arne straightened his cufflinks. "Ready?" he asked.

I looked to Ragnar, who gave me the thumbs-up.

"All right, then," Arne said, and set Sal on his shoulder.

I took the lead, with Ragnar behind me, with Arne and Magnus on either side dazzling the mundanes and handing out business cards.

Magic floated above the seating area outside the Conclave Feast banquet doors. No mundanes came near, and only Mr. Left and Mr. Right stood guard.

Mr. Left pointed. Mr. Right slipped inside.

The "no mundanes" magic around the door left a literal sour taste in my mouth, but Ragnar and I walked up to Mr. Left without setting off elven booby-traps.

"You can't go in there!" Mr. Left held out his hand. Magic formed around his fist. "You're trickster—"

Ragnar wrapped her giant hand around his. "Hush, now, handsome little elf."

I pushed open the Conclave Feast banquet room doors. A curtain of magic hung between me and the elves inside, one that, to the mundanes outside, made the room look like any other corporate meeting.

I swiped my hand through the air, and parted the energy.

The room itself was at least forty feet deep and twenty wide. Protective sigils decorated the bland beige hotel walls. Natural elven magic filled the air along with the rich, savory scent of sage and roasted meats. A hearth filled the center of the large room, complete with flickering fire and crackling logs and a roasting beast on a spit.

Tables circled the hearth and had been moved into a traditional long-table formation, with seating for at least twenty elves on each side. White linens and silver shimmered in the banquet room's lowered lights and flickering candles.

The room teemed with unglamoured elves. What Court sat where, I did not know, only that Tyr Bragisson sat at the head with his wife, Astrid, and their elder both to his right. Dagrun sat to his left, with Niklas der Nord sitting next to her, in what I suspected was Arne's rightful seat.

The room's lights had been dimmed, and candles burned on each table. Silver shimmered, though all tableware looked to be wooden.

They'd built a mini-Great Hall in the center of a Las Vegas hotel, complete with full Viking trappings and a raucous flow of wine and mead.

I walked in, with Ragnar directly behind me. Arne, Sal on his shoulder, followed. Magnus held off the twins.

Half the elves in the room stood. Niklas der Nord jumped out of his chair, one hand out with finger pointing at me, and the other splayed in front of Dagrun as if he thought she needed protecting. "You are not allowed—"

Alfheim's Queen slammed a bowl onto the table. She pushed back her chair so fast it skidded across the carpet. "Sit down, Niklas!" She shoved him away.

"The local Wolf spirit considers itself boss in these parts." I waved my arm at greater Las Vegas. "It has been harassing this troll her entire vacation, correct?"

Ragnar crossed her arms and nodded. "Correct," she said.

"That same spirit attacked me." I held my arm over my head and turned the brand toward the elves.

"You bring trickster magic into the Conclave?" one of the elves yelled.

"I am the jotunn of Alfheim. The Court considers me part of their enclave. Arne Odinsson contains the magic of the brand." Arne's blue-green cuff constricted over the red magic spot on my forearm.

Arne, Sal still on his shoulder, slowly walked along the table. He grinned menacingly at several of the other elves, though he did stop to kiss Astrid Heimdallsdottir's hand.

"Get out!" Niklas der Nord yelled. He turned toward Arne. "No weapons! You have broken—"

In one swift, elegant movement, Arne handed Sal to Tyr Bragisson and hauled Niklas der Nord away from Dagrun. "Quiet, pretender."

"How many of you walk the streets of your enclaves terrified of your local werewolves?" I shouted. "Elves run with the Alfheim Pack at each full moon and help our people continue to be not only stable, but also a major economic force within the community. Any of your elves willing to run with wolves?"

They murmured again.

"I am the cobbled-together son of a mad scientist, yet I am the jotunn of Alfheim." I hit the table. "I was a monster of rage, yet now I stand before an international elven Conclave."

The elves watched each other more than me.

"One of the vampires at the heart of the terror that befell us a week ago was witch-born. He helped me in the end."

The look of shock on Dagrun's face said she had not considered the possibility that Ivan had had a fraction of good in him.

"The vampire's human soul understood the pain my Rose had caused the enclave. He understood the sacrifices they made to help someone not of their kind, and he helped me in return."

The murmur turned into an uproar.

I pointed over my shoulder at Ragnar. "How many of you have antagonized and alienated your local trolls?"

A few of the elves sneered at Ragnar. She pointed at one specific elf. "Your son steals from my rock!" She growled and the elf shrunk down in his seat.

She placed her hand on my shoulder. "The local wolf spirit sent a vampire after me," she said. "This young man offered help. That there is his Troll Killer." She pointed at Sal. "I came anyway."

Ragnar pointed at Magnus. "This one offered a deal." She pointed at Arne. "This one treated me with respect. You lot are worthless, but I will fight for *these* elves."

"A troll," I said. "A creature of your magic whom you ignore has, in the short time the Alfheim Court has been in the hotel, determined that Arne Odinsson's ways are worth her consideration."

"I will fight with the Alfheim elves against the local wolf spirit," Ragnar said.

The elves muttered amongst themselves again.

"The Alfheim Pack stands with the Court of Alfheim," I said. "The jotunn of Alfheim stands with the Court of Alfheim."

"Who here can boast of a stronger enclave economy?" Arne squeezed Dagrun's shoulder. "Who here could field a greater army?"

"Army?" Niklas der Nord bellowed.

He swung at Arne, who dodged.

Arne laughed. "Bears, you say?" He kicked der Nord in the gut.

The Siberian elf staggered backward. He bounced off the wall, but managed to keep his feet under him. He waved his fist at Ragnar. "A *troll*, Odinsson?"

"Fight. Debate. But understand there is a reason you are not the elves in charge of the New Zealand expansion!" I bellowed.

Half the elves jumped to their feet.

Niklas der Nord's lip twitched. "Where's your dog?" he asked.

"Where's your hair?" Magnus shouted.

"This is *not* about me!" Niklas bellowed.

Arne laughed. "You make everything about you. Alfheim business. Iceland business. Vegas business." He slapped his chest and bowed to the table. "It appears you have a busybody in your midst, Olav Sigundsson."

I used to believe that elves were well-behaved when in large groups. That, as one of the old magical breeds, they'd figured out how to communicate like adults. But then I spent time inside The Great Hall.

The elves in the banquet room weren't the stately, serene creatures the mundanes dressed as fake-elves believed them to be. They were loud. They were boisterous. And they liked to brawl as much as they liked to party.

The elven men and women before me were as much Viking warriors as they were magicals, as all their yelling, table pounding, and threats proved.

And Arne and Niklas were about to get into a fist-throwing fight.

The elf who must have been Olav Sigundsson stood up. He slammed his fist into the table and yelled in Russian.

Tyr Bragisson responded, also in Russian. Astrid Heimdallsdottir threw a candle at Sigundsson.

Tyr Bragisson's attention shifted completely to the fight and he set

Sal on the table. Dagrun looked down at my axe, then up at me.

She picked up Sal.

I raised my hand to signal to Ragnar. "Get ready."

The troll nodded and backed toward the door.

Niklas der Nord threw a chair. His magic flared. He lifted his hands, sigils formed, and shoved me. An elf who was a good seven inches shorter than me and whom I outweighed by at least one hundred pounds shoved me hard enough that I stumbled backward.

I don't stumble well. I flounder. I fall. But this time, I had a troll to break my fall.

"Careful, there, not-a-jotunn," she said.

The twins burst through the door and the noise of the concourse poured into the Feast.

Arne responded to der Nord's attack with a bolt of magic so strong it tossed him into the twins—and out the door.

Arne pushed between the twins. "*You* cut off your hair but maiming yourself didn't bring Dagrun back, did it?" he yelled.

They disappeared through the magic and into the realm of the mundanes outside.

Dagrun paid no heed to her husband and her ex. She tilted her head as if listening to Sal, then she nodded.

"You thought hurting yourself would make her feel guilty," Arne yelled outside the door. A flash followed. He must have zapped der Nord again. "Do you think she wouldn't tell me? *I've* been watching you. *You* have burdened my wife!"

Even after three centuries, Niklas felt entitled to Dagrun. Was he like this when they were married? I'd always thought—all of Alfheim thought—that Tyr Bragisson married off his daughter for political reasons, but now I wondered if the situation had been more complicated.

Niklas sure seemed stuck on the past. "You stole *my* wife!" he yelled.

"Niklas der Nord is why we are here!" Dagrun yelled. "All of this," she waved at the banquet room, "could have been handled with a few emails and a conference call. We are the Elven Courts! We are not barbarians. Guidelines could have been set remotely. Expertise offered. Yet here we are out in the open because—"

Dagrun Tyrsdottir turned on her father. "Because you indulged a petty child."

Dag was correct. Arne never threatened the other enclaves. This wasn't a Tov Lokisson moment. All the issues surrounding the vampires could have been handled in a way that strengthened the enclaves, not weakened their infrastructure.

And Alfheim could have offered the same opening-up expertise to everyone else that our elves were bringing to New Zealand.

But no, Niklas der Nord had an old hurt he'd allowed to fester for over three centuries. And that petty festering and its squabbles led directly to the brand on my arm.

Because if this Conclave proved anything, it was that the elves were more concerned about their own brawls than they were about the damage their fights caused to the people and environment around them.

They were Vikings, all right.

"Frank!" Dagrun called.

Astrid Heimdallsdottir was in her husband's face and yelling in Icelandic, with Þórdís Ullrsdottir right at her side.

Dag walked around the tables, twirling Sal around her wrist as she moved. "And here I thought my husband was the crazy one."

She held out Sal.

My axe growled at the red magic on my forearm, and the magic growled right back. They were not compatible—the elven weapon magic that had decided it liked me, and the new, visceral magic that wanted me for a pet.

Dag released Arne's containing band of energy.

Show time, I thought, and grasped Sal with my unbranded arm. "Watch out," I said to Dag, and to Ragnar, "Ready?"

The troll stretched her neck and positioned herself like a baseball catcher between the door and me.

Sal did the elven axe version of an inhale.

I touched the flat side of her blade to the brand.

CHAPTER 24

S al, in her infinite war-weapon wisdom, had made it clear that she did not like my idea for clearing the red magic from my person. The exact impression she'd tossed me had been *don't be an idiot.*

Its removal from my arm wasn't my only goal. I also needed to permanently remove Wolf and its lackeys from my life and Ragnar's in the short amount of time we had left. A violent show of force would work. Arne agreed, even if Sal did not.

She cooperated anyway.

An explosion had resulted the last time Sal touched red magic. This time did not disappoint.

The concussive blast tossed me into Ragnar, and Ragnar through the open doors. We rolled out into the concourse, a rocky troll and a giant with the glowing battle axe, and into the middle of the open-air elven fight.

Sal lay next to me on the concourse carpet, silent and unconscious. My head, and ears, rang with a loud, piercing whine caused by the physical blast and thankfully not by vengeful magic.

Every mundane in the concourse pointed. Der Nord gaped. The twins held back Dag and Magnus, both of whom grinned like kids who'd just won their ball game.

The whine in my ears blocked out Arne's voice. I felt Ragnar's rumble more than heard it. She poked at my arm.

The brand had disconnected from my flesh.

The troll slid her rocky hand over the liquid magic and swept it into her other palm before standing to her full height.

I rolled over onto my back. Nothing felt broken, but my vision blurred and the ringing continued to echo through my ears.

The magic was off. I sighed and looked up at the concourse ceiling.

Ragnar pointed at the elevator lobby.

Every mundane and costumed fake-elf stared as Remy, in full wolf form, trotted into the concourse.

Like me, he and Gerard hadn't started out in the world as beautiful creatures. Old school French *loup-garou* were not the strong, fluffy beasts of modern werewolf lore. They were craven half-man, half-dogs, and horrible to behold.

But the Geroux brothers were men of strong wills, and they had elven help. The Geroux brothers now fully controlled the terms of their transformations.

Full moon, new moon, daylight, whenever—Remy transformed into a huge, fluffy, gunmetal gray North American timber wolf. His snout and the backside of his ears were charcoal. The main body of his tail was also charcoal, and graduated into the black at the tip. His sides were slightly lighter than his back and paws, and in the bright light of the concourse, he appeared to have a saddle much like a German shepherd.

Remy shook his head and his massive ruff fluffed out around his neck. He trotted into the concourse, tongue lolling. He sat, looked over his shoulder, and barked once.

The werewolf wore a red "Service Animal" vest. Remy Geroux, Alpha of the Alfheim Pack, wore the one marker that would keep the mundanes from screaming.

Brilliant, I thought.

Dag knelt at my side. "… concussion…" she said.

"I'll be fine." I rubbed my temple. "I need a moment." My body

178

would right itself soon enough. The ringing, thankfully, diminished to a low squeal fairly quickly. I sat up.

The crowd parted, and Portia Elizabeth also walked out of the elevator lobby. Her dress swirled around her legs and her arms like a gown befitting one of the fake-elves. Her hair was piled high on her head, with tendrils of the dress woven throughout. A generous hood cascaded over her shoulders.

Her green magic flowed around her as great, resonate sheets, but away from Remy—and the elves.

Arne stiffened as she walked toward the elves, and put out his arm to keep der Nord, Magnus, and the twins back.

She smiled only because the situation demanded it. Her mouth may have moved, but her face continued to show suspicion and sadness. "Arne Odinsson," she said. "Your paladin blew himself up."

I rubbed my ears. My head still swam, but I picked out most of her words.

"I got it off, didn't I?" I picked up Sal and forced myself to stand. My axe stayed silent, which was probably for the best. I held her out. "Tell your boss that my elven axe will not tolerate interference or uninvited magic."

Portia Elizabeth's green magic flowed around the mundanes in great oscillating waves. It filled in around the already-calming elven spells, and bolstered their glamours, concealments, and electronics-interfering spells. Everyone in the concourse would remember a show; most of them wouldn't think twice about the lack of video evidence.

Tyr Bragisson appeared in the banquet room's doorway. "What is —" He stopped speaking when he noticed Remy and Portia Elizabeth.

She extended her hand to Ragnar. "I'll take that."

Ragnar held the liquid magic away. "You leave me in peace," she said. "This explosion was a warning. The elves will come for your boss. No more bothering me or the not-a-jotunn."

Portia Elizabeth bowed her head. "I know."

"Promise!" Ragnar barked.

"I cannot promise for Wolf," she said. "Any more than you can."

She wiggled her fingers. "But this," she waved at the crowd, "this is too visible, even with the elven magic. Wolf doesn't like hunting in the open."

Ragnar inhaled. Her rocky skin darkened. She was going to roar at Portia Elizabeth, or swing her fists, or throw scat.

Remy jumped between the two female magicals. He barked and wagged his tail. Then he leaned against Ragnar's leg.

She stared down at the werewolf. "Good wolfie?" she said. "But you old wolfie."

He sat on her foot and pawed at her leg.

Ragnar's stony features visibly softened. She gingerly touched his head.

If Remy could purr, I swear he would have, just to make Ragnar comfortable.

Ragnar smiled. Remy got a troll to smile.

"Good wolfie!" Ragnar plopped down onto the floor. She looked at the red magic on her palm, frowned, and tossed it at Portia Elizabeth.

Remy licked Ragnar's face.

The troll laughed like a little kid. "Good wolfie!"

I stumbled toward Portia Elizabeth. "We can free you, too," I said. The elves could figure out how to use Sal's magic in a way that didn't cause damage. She could be free.

She looked up at my face. "The dress chose me. I chose it. We're symbiotic."

"You don't have to stay in Wolf's employ," I said. "You can—"

She touched my chest. "Remy was right. You are as good as they come, aren't you?"

I didn't know about being "as good as they come," but I did try, no matter how it got me into trouble.

"We can help," I said. "Sal and I can help." Perhaps she was still influencing me. Perhaps not. But she wasn't the dark magical Arne thought her, and I saw no reason for her to suffer.

She touched my cheek. "No offering services to tricksters, Frank Victorsson."

I looked up at the ceiling. Was she a trickster, too? Weren't they all?

She patted my arm, and turned away.

"Portia Elizabeth," I said. "I'm sorry for calling you a, you know…"

She nodded. Her green magic pulled in, and its resonance changed again. It pointed at Niklas der Nord.

Her magic shifted downward at the same time it rose up around der Nord's head. "Before my time in Alfheim, I destroyed men like you. Mundanes, elves, spirits, even a few fae. I consumed them slowly, taking their will, their fortunes, and their reason for living. I spit them out and left only a husk behind."

Portia Elizabeth walked around der Nord. "I chose the bitter." She stroked her finger along his shoulder. "The manipulative and the frightened."

She stopped directly in front of him, with her finger over his heart. "Did that make me a dark magical?"

He stood rigidly, as if she'd turned him to stone.

"Well?" she asked.

He stuck out his chin defiantly. "Yes," he said.

Portia Elizabeth leaned toward him so that her lips were a mere inch from his. "I never found joy in the destruction I caused, yet it was the only cause I knew. Alfheim helped me to widen my worldview."

She kissed him gently. "A lesson you need to learn."

Niklas der Nord gasped.

Portia Elizabeth stepped back. She raised her arms and her dress wavered as if blown by a wind. "Your politics are your own."

Portia Elizabeth flipped her massive hood over her head. She walked to Remy and Ragnar, bowed to the troll, and placed her hand on Remy's ruff. "Red Riding Hood and the Good Wolf!" she declared.

The mundane crowd cheered.

She turned her back to the elves. Remy moved to her side, and they both faced the crowd.

She swung out her arm and took a deep bow. "ElfCon hopes you have enjoyed the show!"

The crowd cheered again. Hoots followed, along with loud chatter.

I waved to Arne. "Take a bow," I mouthed, and gestured, so he'd understand.

He whispered to Dag, who nodded. She spoke to Mr. Left, then took his hand. Within in moments, all the elves near the door were standing in a line—Tyr Bragisson included—like a Broadway show.

They all bowed.

Niklas der Nord frowned. He clenched his fists, and refused to bow. Arne said something to the twins. They nodded.

Mr. Right took Niklas's left elbow, and Mr. Left his right, and escorted him into the banquet room.

Remy trotted over and sat next to my leg. He leaned into me in much the same way Marcus Aurelius leaned against me when he wanted a pet. I responded the same, not really thinking about the fact that I was scratching an Alpha werewolf's ears. Remy snorted and rubbed his head against my hand.

I saw no green magic around him. "You're doing this because you wanted a good Las Vegas story to tell the kids, didn't you?" I asked. "How you played with a troll and were instrumental in saving the day?"

He sneezed and shook his head.

I grinned. "It *is* a good story. Thank you for convincing Portia Elizabeth to come down." Because I was pretty sure her appearance had little to do with me exploding the red magic off my arm and a lot to do with her decision to visit Remy.

Remy winked and trotted to Portia Elizabeth. He leaned against her side, but in a different way than he'd leaned against Ragnar. This time, he meant it.

A dusting of magic washed over them when she placed her hand on his neck.

A couple of fake-elves slowly approached Remy. "That is the biggest dog I have ever seen," the male fake-elf with his fake-blond hair tied up behind his head. This guy wore something that looked more like armor than the regular robes-and-cornet.

Portia Elizabeth smiled, but kept her hand on Remy's neck to signal that the fake-elves were not to touch. "He's part King Shepherd, part Malamute, aren't you, love?"

Remy barked.

"He's gorgeous," the fake-elf said.

"That, he is," she responded.

"What's his name?" The fake-elf was getting much too interested in Remy and might figure out that he wasn't looking at a domesticated dog if we didn't distract him.

Portia Elizabeth didn't look at the fake-elf when she answered. She didn't look at the elves, either. She looked directly at me. "Freki," she said.

Freki and Geri, Odin's wolves. I glanced at Arne as he directed Tyr Bragisson back into the Feast.

When I looked back, she was gone. Just like that, like Batman, she vanished away. The fake-elves didn't seem to realize that they'd been talking to someone who had literally disappeared in front of their eyes.

Remy trotted over to me and sat next to my side as if I were his human and not the woman who'd just disappeared. The fake-elves walked away, oblivious but chatting about ElfCon's "shows."

The concourse's chatter returned to normal. One of the twins appeared and offered to escort Ragnar to the airport, to make sure she arrived at her plane safely. The security spells around the banquet room brightened momentarily, then resettled into "ignore the elves" as all the elves other than Arne filtered back into the Feast.

He waved us over.

"Come in." He stuck his hands into his pockets. The high roller clothes weren't a glamour. He really was dressed in a way that screamed "affluent modern economy" to the other elves. His black, semi-living elven ponytail and the silver tattoos worked surprisingly well with the four-thousand-dollar suit.

I looked out again at where Portia Elizabeth had vanished, then back at Remy's vest. I swore it wasn't the same shade of red it had been a moment ago.

Remy barked and trotted toward the elevators.

"I think he wants to change back to human." I nodded over my shoulder toward the casino. "There might still be fallout from slighting the Las Vegas Wolf spirit."

Arne shrugged. "It knows the elves are now aware."

He was correct, as was Portia Elizabeth—Wolf did not enjoy hunting in the open. We were safe, at least for the moment. "I don't think I will ever come back here," I said.

Arne laughed. "Go on. Help Remy with his Service Dog vest." He laughed again. "We need to get a set for the pack, for emergencies."

And that, right there, was Arne Odinsson, the elven All-Father—setting up contingencies to keep his people safe. As was being the elf with witnesses. And a New Zealand deal.

"Oh," he said, "Magnus is going directly from the Conclave to Auckland."

"Arne," I said. "I'm not flying to New Zealand."

He gripped my arm again. "I think I may ask Þórdís Ullrsdottir. They get along and she might be enough to keep his more intimate relationship-building skills under control."

Someone had to. I motioned toward the elevators. "We'll be back in a few," I said.

Arne turned toward the Feast. "Oskar will let you in when you return."

Oskar must be the twin who stayed to guard the Feast door. I waved and my werewolf friend and I made our way to the elevators for one final clean-up before our official—and no longer necessary—presentation to the Conclave.

At least we'd get a good Las Vegas meal out of it.

CHAPTER 25

The bar shimmered with as many gaudy golds and greens as the rest of the casino. Shadows flitted in the corner booths and between the tables, and the only well-lit part of the floor was the stage area. I sat at the bar proper, a beer in front of me and a lounge act behind.

The singer belted out his rendition of the same pop song Benta had been singing in the shower the morning we left Alfheim for Las Vegas. Turned out it was some mega-hit by a band called Barston Flood. I did my best to ignore the singer's *ohs* and *ahs* while I sipped at my beer.

Remy and I had returned to the Feast and delivered our official speeches to the surprisingly civil elves. Deals were struck. Alliances reformed. Guidelines for how to deal with vampires and other dark magicals hammered out.

The elves talked in hushed tones about Wolf. This development, too, needed hammering. Arne and Dag offered to take point, since the spirit had a particularly American feel.

No one brought up the kitsune. I didn't speak of the two brats while in the banquet room, and figured I'd bring it up privately with Arne and Dagrun when we all returned to Alfheim.

All in all, the Conclave accomplished solidarity. Niklas der Nord had been vanquished by the time Remy and I returned, and the Siberian leadership had already taken a punishment. Tyr Bragisson had clearly lost power among the Courts as well, and Arne and Dagrun had gained.

Portia Elizabeth did not return, nor did the phone-thieving kitsune.

The singer rolled from his rendition of the Barston Flood song to a lounge-lizard cover of Foreigner's "I Want to Know What Love Is."

I picked at my beer bottle. Those two kitsune brats had taken the one connection I had to my mystery woman.

I should have been in my room, sleeping off the whole incident. Remy might be staying in Las Vegas for a few more days, but the elves and I were flying home in the morning. Yet here I sat in the bar, hoping Chip and Lollipop would make one last appearance.

I pulled the label off my beer. The lounge act sang, and I waited.

Wings fluttered. I looked up from my drink.

Raven sat on the stool next to me, her black hair in her two low braids still, wearing a t-shirt, jeans, and an expensive-looking leather biker jacket. "Fashion Santa sure is a bag of dicks," she said.

I almost choked on my beer.

She chuckled. "And now the entirety of the magical world knows to be wary of ponytail-free Siberian elves." When the bartender came over, she pointed at my beer. "I'll have what he's having."

All the Courts were now well aware of der Nord's proclivities. He'd lost power because of it. They were also now aware of Las Vegas Wolf.

I watched Raven arrange her napkin. "We have a microbrewery in Alfheim," I said. "Raven's Gaze, they call it. It's run by a couple of elves." I took a swig, then held out my bottle. "Come for the beer. Stay for the magic."

Raven smiled. "Sounds worth a try."

I set down my beer. "Remy says he'll be home in a week or two." I'd honestly expected him to stay. House would take him in, at least temporarily.

She thanked the bartender when he set down her beer. "Wolf won't bother him." She took a swig.

"What about Portia Elizabeth? After what I saw at Crossroads, a punishment seems likely."

"That dress of hers, it's not Wolf's magic." Raven took a swig of her beer. "Portia Elizabeth was working for Wolf before the dress showed up. Dealing with Wolf's issues helps her channel her dark tendencies."

Which made sense. I sipped my own beer.

Raven tapped her bottle on the bar and stared at her fingers. "She and that dress, they have a deal. Portia Elizabeth will be fine."

Her body language suggested she didn't believe what she'd just said —or that she had an understanding of Portia Elizabeth's "deal."

"Alfheim will take her," I said. For Remy, at least.

Raven shook her head. "She can't, Frank. She can't be around the men of Remy's pack, especially his nephew."

"Jaxson? He's a kid." Raven wasn't making sense. Fertility spirits only affected the fertile.

But then again, Portia Elizabeth wasn't a random fertility spirit.

Raven sipped her beer. "How do you think her powers interact with fated mate magic?"

"Not well?" But then, I was pretty sure I saw fated mate magic flowing between her and Remy.

"Two weeks, three tops, and *all* males... react... even with her dress suppressing her magic. She refuses to risk it. Not with kids."

Which meant that Remy wouldn't be staying beyond two weeks, either.

"What is that dress? The red magic?" I asked.

Raven turned around and leaned against the bar just as the lounge act started up with yet another cover of a well-known love song. "No one knows who made it, or its true purpose." She shrugged. "Every so often, something unexpected shows up at Crossroads. It's part of its charm."

"Charm?" I wouldn't call such mysterious magic charming.

Raven shook her head. Then she tapped the bar and pulled a business card out of her jacket. "The concealments around House extend to our persons, and thus our business dealings, which was why you didn't find Portia Elizabeth with a simple Internet search."

And why Remy never found her in all his years searching.

I took the card. *Elizabeth Portman, arbiter and therapist*, it said, followed by a string of degree and licensing letters, and a phone number.

"Three quarters of her clients are men. She fixes them up and sends them back into the world." Raven pushed her napkin around. "She's built a life here."

"Impressive," I said.

"She is also licensed to perform weddings." Raven grinned. "So am I."

I laughed. "It *is* Vegas."

The address on the card was an office, not an apartment at House. "Does House always mess with time? How does anyone live there?" Three days was a lot to lose when one had to get to work the next morning.

"That was all me, handsome." Raven leaned against the bar. "How do wolves hunt?" she asked.

"They separate their prey from the herd," I answered.

Raven touched her finger to her nose, then pointed at me. "I was not about to let my prize service-offering hound be separated from his pack."

She stole three days to make sure I didn't start hunting for Ragnar until the elves arrived? Maybe I wasn't just a shiny, new bauble with which to play.

"Your expression, yet again, tells me all I need to know." She sipped her beer.

I tucked Portia Elizabeth's card into my pocket. "I take it I learned whatever lesson you wished me to learn?" What else could she "need to know?"

Raven laughed. "The question is not what *you* learned, but what *I* learned from your process of learning."

"I hope I did not disappoint," I said.

"No, Mr. Victorsson, you did not." Raven took a sip. "We'll send Remy home in one piece."

"I'm sure you will." Hoped they would.

"Oh!" Raven reached into her impossible pocket again. "The kitsune asked me to give this to you."

She held out my phone.

I took it. The kitsune gave Raven my phone?

"You are released from your offer of service, son of Victor." She bowed her head.

"Thank you?" I said. She'd traded my offer to Wolf, so I wasn't as sure of my release as she seemed to be.

I unlocked the screen. "Did they booby-trap it?" Chip and Lollipop did like their tricks.

She shook her head and tipped her beer toward my phone. "It's clean of any trick magic. I checked."

The woman in the phone still hugged my dog, still beautiful, still a little sad, and still a mystery.

Raven pulled a one-hundred-dollar bill from her pocket. "I'm glad I met you, Frank Victorsson."

"I'm glad I met you, too," I said absently. Though I was more ambivalent about Raven the trickster than I'd tell her to her face.

I swiped at my phone to move to my second screen of apps. Right in the middle of my phone's screen, bigger than any of the other app icons, was a lollipop.

"Do you know what this is?" I showed my phone to Raven.

"The one with the mutant tastebuds said, 'Tell him we agree to his terms.'"

"That's it?" What terms were they talking about?

Raven shrugged. "Are you going to open the app?" She slipped the hundred-dollar bill under her beer bottle.

What if my phone exploded? Because I wouldn't put it past those two brats to set my life literally on fire, no matter if the Raven World Spirit checked it over or not.

Raven stood up. "Open it. See what they have to say." She squeezed my shoulder. "I suspect it's not so bad."

With that, the magical who was much more than she let on walked toward the bar's door.

I looked down at my phone. I might as well dive in. I tapped the lollipop.

My phone's screen went white, and for an uncomfortably long moment, nothing happened. Did those brats wipe my phone?

Japanese text appeared. "I can't read this," I muttered. It scrolled and scrolled, then stopped on a line of English. *We will make contact when the need arises*, it said.

The scrolling Japanese was probably a contract of some sort. I'd need to be extra careful, especially until I could get it translated.

But then a phone icon appeared, and an international number. My phone was dialing Japan.

Should I end the call? Allowing a connection probably meant I accepted whatever terms were laid out in the Japanese text.

Unless this was how I got information about my mystery woman. I inhaled, and put the phone to my ear. The line clicked, and clicked, and finally rang.

A woman answered. *"Kon'nichiwa?"*

Was it her? I didn't think so. Not at a Japanese phone number.

"Umm, hello," I said. "My name is Frank Victorsson. You might find this hard to believe, but two kitsune gave me this number."

"Kitsune?" she said.

"One likes potato chips. The other lollipops."

"Ah," she responded. "Yes. They told me you would call."

"They did?" Maybe this woman knew something. "Did they tell you why?"

"Mr. Victorsson," the woman said. "My name is Chihiro Hatanaka. That woman in the photo on your phone? Her name is Ellie Jones. She and her cottage disappeared from my *kougai* a week ago. She is my best friend."

"Ellie Jones?" I said. *Yes*, I thought. *Ellie*. Her name was Ellie and she was the most wonderful person I'd ever met.

The woman named Chihiro Hatanaka inhaled sharply. "You forget her."

"I do." *Concealment enchantments*, I thought. It had to be enchantments. "How do I stop the forgetting?"

"There is a way," Chihiro Hatanaka said. "Mr. Victorsson, I can help you find Ellie Jones."

EPILOGUE

S omewhere in the gritty fog infesting the borderland hell, a vampire wailed. They prowled out there, the more idiotic of Lord Dracula's children, feeding on each other and concentrating their toxic blood.

Most understood the warning barrier around his pit and backed away before he caught a glimpse of a pale limb or a red eye. Every so often, one did stumble near and kick debris into his hole, and dust would rain down onto his head.

Sooner or later, one would come too close and fall in. They were soldiers without a general, the howling vampires above, and the pathetic fights to fill the power vacuum would likely lead to an idiot or two tripping during a scuffle.

The small, hunched vampire who had regained his soul—Ivan, his name was—occasionally leaned over the pit's edge and stared in quiet contemplation. They never exchanged words. Then the Souled One vanished once again into the fog.

He did not remember his own name, though he knew it was not Lord Dracula, nor was it Brother. His body might have been stitched together by the same madman who stitched together Frank Victorsson, but he would not bedevil the man with a fraternal claim ever again.

He could, at least in that small way, redeem himself.

He did remember Lord Dracula's will and desires, and his solidified ragings. He also remembered the bitter, cold gamesmanship of the personality that called itself Brother. That personality had wanted to be the winner, but of what, he did not understand.

There were other personalities in this body with him, all vampires, all consumed by a cold-as-death need to steal life. It was a force of the universe unto itself, this need to suck away energy and reason.

Was he a vampire? His new body had been built of vampire parts. All the demons dancing its edges were vampires.

Magic still coiled around him, still flitted and touched and boiled inside the now-inert armor he still wore, but access had been taken from him. His magic—the intrinsic magic of his cobbled-together form—wanted nothing to do with the mind who now steered its arms, legs, hands, and feet.

Yet here he was, a man who had broken fingers, ripped out nails, and destroyed joints digging bare-handed through the stone walls of a now long-gone prison—a man wrongly incarcerated for a murder he did not commit—digging yet again.

Had he gotten out of his first prison? Was this his afterlife? Was being the only mundane man inside an eight-foot-tall walking vampire his eternal torment?

No, there was an outside. Brother walked it for close to two centuries. Dracula yearned to ravish it and burn it to nothing. The other vampires wanted to feed on its living corpse.

So he dug. The cutting end of the remains of Dracula's pike bit into the gravel and dust at the floor of his hell. It sliced through the dry, hard-packed ash. It broke through layers and layers of dust and death. He'd dug down a good twelve feet already.

There had to be a bottom. This pocket curled in on itself—he had walked for what felt like months only to find his marker again—but even a curled ribbon had an edge. There had to be a way through the layers.

He would not give up his one real hope. There had to be a way out. There *had* to be.

He raised his arms over his head, breathed in the foul air, and slammed the pike into the shale-like dryness under his feet. Radial cracks snapped though the solid gray, brittle not-quite-stone and echoed off the sides of his pit. Dust puffed, and gravel rattled down the sides.

These pieces were larger than many others, and even. He'd add them to his steps he'd cut into the side of his pit, the ones he used to transport debris to the barrier.

Up above, vampires shrieked. Sounds of a scuffle followed, and the wet thudding of a body broken on his rubble pile.

Then nothing. No shuffling. No footfalls. No disturbances in the ceaseless and sulfuric fog.

He rubbed his eyes and peered up at the edges of his pit.

Black fabric fluttered in the roiling fog. It reached out over the pit, then gently drifted down to drape over the dusty wall.

He could not tell the true color of the fabric's blackness. Was it so empty it reflected nothing but the void? Did it hold in its threads all possible colors, thus projecting everything at once? Was the black obsidian, and shiny? Did a subtle rainbow dance through it as if it were ink?

It was all, yet it was not.

A blackness-clad leg appeared, then another. Then the legs' owner leaned forward.

Sweet platinum curls cascaded around the woman's youthful, round face. A rosy glow brightened her babyish cheeks. Brilliantly violet eyes blinked as she tipped her head. Her large breasts heaved over her knees as she looked down at him, and she also carried more heft and abundant thickness to her than he expected on a vampire.

Her smile was also much warmer and alive than he expected.

"Hi!" she called. "My name's Anthea. Would you like some company down there?"

He set down Dracula's pike. "No," he said.

She pouted. "Ah, don't be that way." The black fabric of her dress coiled up her neck and into her hair, and pulled the curls away from her face. "We're all stuck here, you know. Why not keep each other company?"

She wasn't like any of the other vampires. Not at all.

"Go away," he said. He didn't need an odd vampire taking up room in his pit.

"Now, see, here's the thing." She leaned over again, and banged her heels against the pit's wall. "My dress is telling me that all the magic of this place emanated from you, or at least that body." She waved her hand through the fog. "There's another here, someone with a soul. He helped with all this. I can't find him." She looked down again. "I've been looking."

She most definitely was different.

"I came through the gate because of Lord Dracula's call." She shook her head. "My dress is angry. It thinks I should have been able to resist, but sometimes I'm not as strong as my sisters."

Power radiated off the black fabric as if it was magic—not enchanted. Not an artifact, but a physical, visceral magic in and of itself.

He stepped closer to her swinging toes. "What are you?" he asked.

She smiled again. "I'm a vampire, silly. Can I come down? The nice thing to do is to invite me in."

"No," he said. "You stay there." He wasn't about to invite any vampire into the one way out of this pocket borderland hellscape.

Anthea pouted again. "But you're big and strong and it's scary up here." The magic of the black dress tightened around her throat. Her mouth rounded, and she blinked. "Oh," she said.

The dress did something. It corrected her somehow.

"My dress wants me to tell you that I am more than capable of taking care of myself up here. It wants me to remember that I *am* a vampire, even if all I ever wanted was to be a singer." She leaned over again. "It doesn't like it when I do that."

"Do what?" he asked.

She waved her fingers in front of her face. "Be manipulative. It chose me because I can be good." She smiled again. "I tutor the neighborhood kids. Help them audition. Work with them on getting an agent. All that."

She tutored children?

"Yeah," she said. "It's weird. I know. But the dresses, they're sick of being harbingers, you know? Ushering in apocalypses is sort of depressing. They're not really needed anymore, either. Not with the Internet. So they're looking to move up in the magical world. Become something new. Adapt or die, you know. So they chose us, the dark ones who can be good, to help them with their retraining."

She grinned and her vampire fangs shimmered. "My sisters, they want to be good. Their dresses like that. My dress has to remind me every so often that I'm along for the ride, but I don't mind. Sometimes the whole evil vampire thing as is as depressing and boring as being a harbinger."

She grinned again. "Do you ever think about that? How *boring* it is to be a regular vampire? I miss the sun."

His instincts were to run, but he was in his pit, and had not yet uncovered a true escape route.

She blinked her lovely violet eyes. "My dress says it can help with the digging. It wants out of here just as much as you do."

"What *are* you?"

She raised her hands over her head and her lovely breasts thrust forward. "Not what *am* I, silly! What I'm going *to be*. I'm going to get you out of here," she said. "I'm your guide and you're my first client. My dress and I, we're auditioning for a new job."

He picked up the pike and backed against the wall.

"We're going to take you to Valhalla," she said. "Because I'm going to be a valkyrie."

GET FREE BOOKS

SUBSCRIBE TO KRIS AUSTEN RADCLIFFE'S NEWSLETTER

You will be notified when Kris Austen Radcliffe's next novel is released, as well as gain access to an occasional free bit of author-produced goodness. Your email address will never be shared and you can unsubscribe at any time.

WWW.SIXTALONSIGN.COM/MAILING-LIST-SIGN-UP/

THE WORLDS OF
KRIS AUSTEN RADCLIFFE

Smart Urban Fantasy:

Northern Creatures

Monster Born

Vampire Cursed

Elf Raised

Wolf Hunted

Fae Touched

Death Kissed

God Forsaken

Magic Scorned

Witch Burned (*coming soon*)

Northern Creatures Box Set One: Books 1-3

Northern Creatures Box Set Two: Books 4-6

Genre-bending Science Fiction about

love, family, and dragons:

WORLD ON FIRE

Series one

Fate Fire Shifter Dragon

Games of Fate

Flux of Skin

Fifth of Blood

Bonds Broken & Silent

All But Human

Men and Beasts

The Burning World

Dragon's Fate and Other Stories

Series Two

Witch of the Midnight Blade: The Complete Series

Series Three

<u>World on Fire</u>

Call of the Dragonslayer (*coming soon*)

Hot Contemporary Romance:

<u>The Quidell Brothers</u>

Thomas's Muse

Daniel's Fire

Robert's Soul

Thomas's Need

Quidell Brothers Box Set

Includes:

Thomas's Muse

Daniel's Fire

Roberts's Soul

ABOUT THE AUTHOR

Kris's Science Fiction universe, **World on Fire**, brings her descriptive touch to the fantastic. Her Urban Fantasy series, **Northern Creatures**, sets her magic free. She's traversed many storytelling worlds including dabbles in film and comic books, spent time as a talent agent and a textbook photo coordinator, as well written nonfiction. But she craved narrative and richly-textured worlds—and unexpected, true love.

Kris lives in Minnesota with one husband, two daughters, and three cats.

For more information
www.krisaustenradcliffe.com

www.ingramcontent.com/pod-product-compliance
Lightning Source LLC
Chambersburg PA
CBHW060927180626
46817CB00004B/1430